MOTHER'S DAY

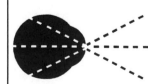

This Large Print Book carries the
Seal of Approval of N.A.V.H.

MOTHER'S DAY

HEARTACHE MATURES INTO LASTING LOVE IN THIS ROMANTIC STORY

JOYCE LIVINGSTON

THORNDIKE PRESS
A part of Gale, Cengage Learning

GALE
CENGAGE Learning™

Detroit • New York • San Francisco • New Haven, Conn • Waterville, Maine • London

GALE
CENGAGE Learning

Copyright © 2005 by Joyce Livingston.
Scripture quotations are taken from the King James Version of the Bible.
Thorndike Press, a part of Gale, Cengage Learning.

Thorndike Press® Large Print Christian Fiction.
The text of this Large Print edition is unabridged.
Other aspects of the book may vary from the original edition.
Set in 16 pt. Plantin.
Printed on permanent paper.

LIBRARY OF CONGRESS CATALOGING-IN-PUBLICATION DATA

Livingston, Joyce.
    Mother's day : heartache matures into lasting love in this romantic story / by Joyce Livingston.
        p. cm. — (Thorndike Press large print Christian fiction)
    (Rhode Island weddings : bk. 2)
    ISBN-13: 978-1-4104-1392-5 (alk. paper)
    ISBN-10: 1-4104-1392-6 (alk. paper)
    1. Large type books. I. Title.
PS3562.I9435C65 2009
813'.54—dc22   2008051227

Published in 2009 by arrangement with Barbour Publishing, Inc.

Printed in the United States of America
1 2 3 4 5 6 7 13 12 11 10 09

DEDICATION

The very day I finished writing *Mother's Day,* the news of the abduction of an eleven-year-old girl flashed across the television screen. A security camera on a car wash actually captured her abductor grabbing on to her arm and dragging her away. Though he was apprehended a day or two later, the girl wasn't found for over a week. I shuddered as I watched in horror the day they found her body. That could have been one of my granddaughters. Or maybe your daughter or granddaughter. The world is filled with those who would do our children harm. We must be diligent in watching them and training them not only how to keep themselves aware and avoid situations that could put them in jeopardy, but how to defend themselves against such perverts. If you see anything suspicious or have any information about a missing child, please report it as quickly as possible by calling 1-800-THE-LOST. Your tip may save a child's life.

CHAPTER ONE

Chuck O'Connor stormed through the door of the house on Victor Lane, slamming it behind him and tossing his set of keys onto the highly polished hall table with a loud thud.

Mindy, who was sorting through the day's mail, spun around to face her husband, ready to scold him for his careless act. But the look on his face told her something was radically wrong. Although she had seen his angry side many times during their troublesome fourteen-year marriage, she had never seen his hands tremble or his face so flushed. She hurriedly placed the mail on the coffee table and rushed toward him. "What's wrong?"

Chuck yanked off his coat, tossed it on a chair instead of hanging it in the closet, as was his usual behavior, and pushed past her with a grunt.

She planted her balled fists on her hips.

"Chuck! Are you going to tell me or sulk all by yourself?"

He snatched up the mail and began sorting through it, dropping several envelopes on the floor in the process.

Her patience wearing thin, Mindy crossed the room and yanked on his sleeve, her own anger rising. "All right, don't tell me then," she told him in a stern voice, holding up her hands between them with a frown of frustration.

Tossing the mail back on the table, Chuck plopped his lanky body onto the sofa, fixing his elbows on his knees and cradling his head in his hands. "Jake suspended me."

Thinking surely she had misunderstood his barely audible words, Mindy sat down beside him, placing a hand on his shoulder. "Jake suspended you? I find that hard to believe. You do everything by the book. You're always the top one in sales. Why would he suspend you?"

Chuck sat stone still and didn't respond, his head still resting in his hands, but his rapid breathing told her his anger had not subsided.

"Chuck?" she said softly, gently rotating her fingers across his tense shoulders. "Don't shut me out. I'm your wife. You know you can tell me anything. Why did your boss suspend you?"

Swallowing hard, he slowly lifted his face to meet hers. "You may not want to be my wife when I tell you."

She gave him a puzzled look. Whatever could he mean? They'd had some pretty rocky years, come close to divorce more times than she cared to remember, but they'd struggled through each problem and stayed together. What could be worse than anything they had faced in the past?

"I've" — he paused, still covering his face and pressing his fingertips against his lowered eyelids — "I've been accused of molesting someone."

Mindy stared at him. "What? You? Molesting someone? That doesn't make any sense." She scooted closer, her hand still resting on his back, her fingers splayed. "Who accused you?"

Slowly Chuck pulled his hands away and, with misty eyes, turned to face her. "Jake called me into his office and told me. It — it was one of the women employees. Michelle Stevens."

Mindy tried hard to put a face to the name. Had she met this woman at the company Christmas party? "Is that the little bimbo in the accounting department? The one with the bleached-blond ponytail and

9

the false fingernails?"

He shook his head. "No, Michelle is nothing like that. She's — plain. Kinda ordinary. Has short brown hair and wears glasses."

"Why would she do such a thing? I don't even remember your mentioning her name."

Chuck leaned back and locked his hands behind his head, staring off into space. "I — I never did."

"Chuck? Why?" Mindy's heart sank. "Was something going on between you two?"

His brows quickly furrowing, he glared at her. "Of course not! How can you even ask me that?"

She shrugged, then let out a sigh. "Something must have happened between the two of you to get Jake that riled up. Why else would she make such a statement?"

Though Chuck only lifted his shoulders in response, something about the look on his face gave her cause for alarm. In all the years they'd been married, they'd had problems — many problems — but infidelity had never been one of them. Surely not now — not when their lives had finally settled down into a compatible routine. "Chuck! I asked you a question. I think I deserve an explanation. What did Jake say?"

"It's not true, Mindy. I swear it! It's not true."

She grabbed tightly on to his wrist. "Are you going to tell me what Jake said, or am I going to have to call and ask him myself? I will, you know."

His long fingers clamped her hand. They felt warm. Almost feverish.

"Okay. Let me start at the beginning." He pulled his hand away, rose, and began pacing slowly about the room. "Jake called me into his office, and we talked for over half an hour about business, his family, my family, where we planned to go on vacation this year — all sorts of things that really didn't matter. I could tell he had something on his mind, but I had no idea what. Finally, he leaned across his desk and pointed his finger in my face and asked point-blank if I was having an affair with Michelle."

She blanched at his words. "What did you say? Are you?"

He rammed his fist into the palm of his other hand, glaring at her. "No! I answered an unequivocal no! Of course I wasn't having an affair with Michelle! I told him that."

"Apparently he didn't believe you. He suspended you!" she shot back, half-wishing she had kept her silence until he finished his story.

His eyes flashed. "Hey, where's the trust a wife's supposed to have for her husband?

11

You haven't even heard me out, and you're already finding me guilty," he countered, his voice rising.

"I never said —"

"But you implied it. That's just as bad." He lowered himself into a chair opposite her and, gripping the arm rests, bent toward her, his face contorted with anger. "Now do you want to hear the whole story or not?"

Annoyed by his patronizing behavior and with her heart pounding, she nodded. "Yes, I'm sorry. Go on."

"It appears that Dixie, one of the secretaries in the sales department, was in a stall in the ladies' restroom when Michelle came in and called someone on her cell phone, not realizing Dixie was there. She told whoever she was talking to that she had a new boyfriend and mentioned his name was Chuck but cautioned them to keep it quiet because the man was married. Then when she discovered Dixie was there, she begged her not to tell anyone about the conversation she'd overheard."

Mindy could not help letting out a gasp but kept her silence when Chuck frowned.

"I guess Dixie told everyone."

"Did Dixie or anyone else tell Jake what she'd heard?" Mindy asked cautiously.

"No. Not then. Not until after he talked

to Michelle."

Mindy frowned. If Dixie hadn't told Jake, why would Jake talk to Michelle about it?

"I guess I'm not making myself clear." Chuck sent her a weak smile. "This thing has me so upset I'm not thinking straight." He gave his head a frustrated shake, then continued. "Michelle went to Jake early this morning and told him I'd molested her. That's what this is all about."

"Why would she say such a thing?"

"I don't know."

"She had to have said something convincing enough for him to suspend you."

"The sad thing is, he put me on suspension but let her keep her job! Some justice, huh?" The two sat silently staring at one another. There was so much Mindy wanted to know, but she refrained from asking, sure her questions would throw Chuck into a tirade. If he was innocent, he had every right to some righteous indignation. If he was guilty, any words she hurled at him would only fan the flames.

Finally, Chuck turned to face her again, taking her hands in his. "I didn't do it, Mindy. I know at times I have a hot temper and I let it get the best of me, but I'd never hurt a woman in any way. You know that. Over the years we've been together, you've angered me to the boiling point a number of times, but I've never struck you or laid a hand on you."

"Are — are you saying she accused you of hitting her? That kind of molesting?"

Chuck gave a sad shake of his head. "No, the other kind."

"Chuck! This is like a bad dream! Why would she accuse you of something like that if it weren't true?"

He glowered at her, his face flushed and his fists clenched. "So you believe it, too, eh?"

"I — I didn't say that."

"You didn't? It sounded that way to me!"

Mindy bit her tongue, trapping the words that nearly slipped from her mouth, a retort that would have angered him even more.

"I never — let me repeat — I never molested that woman — in any way!"

"I — I can't imagine that you would. Tell me the rest. What happened after Jake asked you about her?" Mindy prodded gently.

"According to her story, I had come on to her, invited her to drive up to Providence and have dinner with me a few times, and things got pretty heavy between us. She even claimed I told her you and I were getting a divorce."

"A divorce? We haven't talked about a

14

divorce for four years!"

He patted her hand. "I know. She went on to say she had decided to break things off between us. She also said that one night after we'd been to dinner in Providence and gone back to her apartment, she told me she was calling it quits and I got really mad. She claims" — he paused and pursed his lips — "she claims I slapped her around, then made advances on her, and when she refused I — I raped her."

Mindy's hands flew to cover her face. "Oh, no, no, no, no! I can't believe this is happening!"

Chuck held her arms so tightly she squealed in pain. "I didn't, Mindy. I swear it! None of this ever happened."

Mindy felt sick to her stomach. "You never drove that woman to Providence like she said?"

He shook his head vehemently. "Not one time!"

"Then why, Chuck? Why?"

"That's the same thing Jake asked me."

Fighting back a stream of tears and feeling light-headed, Mindy sucked in a cleansing breath of air. "I find it difficult to believe she would make up a story like this and then just waltz into Jake's office and tell him!"

Chuck braced an elbow on one knee, cupping his chin in his hand. "Jake said he had a hard time believing it, too. And though he wasn't completely convinced she was telling the truth, he said he had no choice but to put me on suspension until her accusations could be proved or disproved. It's a serious charge. I'm well aware of that. To make things worse, Dixie verified the restroom cellphone conversation."

Mindy dropped to her knees in front of Chuck, lifting her face to his and gripping his hands. "Look me in the eye, Chuck, and tell me none of this is true."

Her husband of fourteen years trembled. Finally, his eyes filling with tears and his voice breaking, he answered. "Some — some of it is sort of true."

CHAPTER TWO

"Sort of true?" Mindy quickly released his hands and rocked back on her heels, wanting to distance herself from him as much as possible. "Some of it is sort of true, Chuck? Exactly what does that mean?"

"Don't get upset until you hear me out."

Mindy stood quickly to her feet and jutted out her chin. "I'm beginning to think I've heard too much already. How could you do this to us, Chuck? To our family? You're not even old enough to be having a midlife crisis!"

Chuck grabbed her forearm and held on fast. "I did take her to dinner once, but that was right here in town, and only because I felt sorry for her."

"You never told me about it!" she screamed back at him, feeling betrayed.

He released his hold and threw his hands up in the air. "Because I knew you'd react just like you're doing right now!"

Mindy stomped her foot. "And you wouldn't behave the same way if I told you I'd been out playing footsie with some guy?"

"We weren't playing footsie!"

Mindy leaned toward him, her hands on her hips. "Then what were you doing, Chuck? Tell me that!"

He sucked in a breath and let it out slowly. "A couple of months ago when you drove to Bristol to visit that friend of yours —"

"While the cat's away, the mice will play, huh?" She was sorry she said it the minute it slipped out.

Chuck spun around and headed toward the kitchen, leaving her standing there, feeling terrible.

Swallowing her pride, she followed him. After pouring them each a cup of the coffee she had put on to brew just before he got home, she handed his cup to him, adding a quiet "I'm sorry. That remark was uncalled for."

He took the cup and seated himself on a stool at the breakfast bar. "It was raining when I drove out of the parking garage, and there was Michelle, standing at the bus stop looking as if she'd lost her best friend. I stopped and asked her what was wrong. She said she'd missed her bus, and another one wouldn't be along for another forty-five minutes. I hated to drive off and leave her there, so I offered to take her home. I guess I mentioned it wouldn't make any difference if I got home later than usual, because you were out of town and my daughter was staying overnight at a friend's house and I'd be fixing supper for myself."

"And she came up with this brilliant idea to fix supper for you in her apartment!" Mindy harangued sarcastically, tilting her head at a haughty angle.

Chuck looked as though he would like to choke her. "No, Miss Know-It-All, it wasn't anything like that. She simply offered to buy my supper at a little diner not far from her place."

"And being the gentleman, you took her up on it, right?"

He nodded, the incensed expression never leaving his face. "I couldn't see any harm in it — at the time. Now I know better."

"It must have been cozy. Sounds like something from an old movie. The rain. The diner. The gallant hero who rescues the damsel in jeopardy." Mindy knew her voice had a denigrating tone, but she didn't care. The whole thing upset her, and he needed to know it.

Chuck slammed his cup down, knocking the carton of coffee cream over, splattering it across the countertop. "Think what you like, Mindy. I'm only going to say this one more time. I don't care what that woman says. There was never anything between us."

"You have told me the whole story, haven't you, Chuck?"

He slid off the stool, his dark eyes menacing. "Why should I tell you? You've already tried and convicted me. I can see it in your eyes."

"So?" She turned away and tossed a couple of paper napkins onto the stream of cream that was slowly making its way across the counter. "I think you'd better move into the guest room until this thing is settled. I — I can't imagine sharing a bed with a man —" She stopped midsentence.

"A man you don't trust? Is that it, Mindy? Our years together don't mean anything to you? You're willing to cast me aside, just because a stranger tells a lie about me?"

"A lie? How do I know it's a lie? I'd like to believe you, Chuck — you know I would — but you just told me there was more to the story! I'm afraid to think how much more! I'm only asking you to move into the guest room until this thing is cleared up."

Chuck moved toward the door, his shoulders drooping, and leaned against the doorframe. "I — I guess, if I was honest, I'd admit I'd feel exactly the way you do. I was pretty shaken when Jake told me what she'd said. I knew it wasn't true, but how could I expect you to react any differently when you have only my word for it?" He fingered the slight growth of stubble on his chin, as if debating what to say next. "I'm sorry for blowing up at you, Mindy. I guess, under the circumstances, your request is reasonable. I'll move into the guest room as you've asked. Perhaps it would be best."

"How will we explain it to Bethany?" she asked, suddenly realizing their nearly thirteen-year-old daughter would be coming home soon.

He stroked his forehead thoughtfully. "Since she's usually in bed before we are, she won't even notice. I'll set my alarm a half hour earlier, so I'll already be up when she gets up. No need to get her involved in this."

"Thanks. I sure don't want to upset her. I doubt she's forgotten all the arguments we used to have when she was younger. I think it'd be best if we kept all this to ourselves. I don't want her worrying about it." Mindy walked slowly toward him. "Want me to help you move things?"

He gave his head a sad shake. "No thanks. I can do it myself." With that he turned and

21

disappeared through the kitchen doorway.

Mindy watched him go, feeling as if her world had just collapsed around her. Though Chuck had never been a model husband, he had been a model father. It would not be fair to shake Bethany's trust in him since, she hoped, he would soon be proven innocent and things would get back to normal.

She moved to the sink and wet a clean dishcloth under the faucet, then robotically began to clean up the spilled cream.

Mindy froze when she heard the front door open. Had Chuck decided to leave? Maybe take a motel room somewhere? She hoped not. After all, this was his home, too, and that's where he needed to be.

"Hi, Mom!" a voice called out cheerily.

"In the kitchen!" Mindy dabbed at her eyes with the dish towel. "You're home early!"

Her pretty daughter bolted into the kitchen and plopped her books onto the counter. "The game ended early. Where's Dad? I saw his car in the driveway. He's home early, too. Does that mean we can go out for pizza for supper?"

"I — I don't know. Your —"

"I'm right here, Princess." Chuck strode into the room and wrapped his long arms around his daughter, planting a kiss on her forehead. "Pizza sounds fine to me, if it's okay with your mother."

Mindy forced a smile, glad Bethany hadn't wandered into her bedroom before coming into the kitchen and found her father preparing to move his things into the guest room. "Pizza it is!"

Though she felt awkward sitting close to her husband in the crowded restaurant, Mindy did her best to keep their conversation light, making small talk about things that had happened at her office that morning and about an article she had read in a women's magazine about raising teenagers. "You'll be a teenager in a few weeks," she reminded her daughter.

Bethany grinned at her mom, then turned to her dad. "Just think, Dad — I can get my learner's permit next year, and you can teach me how to drive."

Chuck rolled his eyes. "I can hardly wait."

"Dad!" Bethany slapped at his arm. "Some of my friends' fathers are already teaching them to drive."

His eyes rounded. "Not on the street, I hope!"

"Well, not exactly drive, but they're letting them start the car and move it back and forth in the driveway."

Chuck laughed. "Hey, the last thing I need is a big hole in the garage door. I think you'd better wait until you're fourteen and it's legal. Then I'll take you to a big parking lot sometime when all the stores are closed and let you behind the wheel." He jabbed her arm playfully. "Better yet, why don't you just wait until you can take the driver's education class at your school?"

Bethany wiped a string of cheese from her father's chin. "What's the matter, Dad? You afraid I'll wreck that old Corvette of yours?"

"The thought did cross my mind."

Mindy watched the two of them, and despite the bombshell Chuck had dropped on her only hours earlier, she had to smile. If there was one thing she could never accuse him of, it was being a less-than-perfect father. Though she and her husband had disagreed on practically everything about Mindy's upbringing since even before she was born, Chuck had always had their daughter's best interests at heart. He had been there for all of it and had been an integral part of Bethany's life in every way.

"Isn't that right, Mom?"

Brought out of her thoughts by her daughter's question, Mindy gave her a blank stare. "What? What did you say? I'm sorry — I had other things on my mind." She could not help but glance in Chuck's direction.

Bethany let out a giggle. "I said Daddy was funny! Didn't you hear his joke?"

"No — I guess I didn't."

"It wasn't that funny, Princess," Chuck said, giving Mindy a shy grin. "Hey, now that we've finished our pizza, how about an ice cream cone? Maybe Rocky Road or Pralines and Cream?"

Bethany leaped to her feet and grabbed her jacket from the back of her chair after tweaking her father's cheek between her fingers. "Or Peppermint Crunch, your favorite, Dad!"

Chuck reached out his hand to Mindy. "That okay with you?"

She nodded and smiled back, but inwardly her heart was breaking. *Oh, Chuck. Sweet, sweet Chuck. Am I crazy to doubt you?*

Later that night as Mindy lay in their bed, her head propped up on a pillow, trying to get her mind off their problems by reading a romance novel, she heard the grandfather clock in the hall chime eleven times, then footsteps in the hall. Chuck was on his way to bed. She ran her hand across the empty pillow beside her, remembering years past, miserable years for both of them, when he had spent much of his time in that guest room. She held her breath, half-hoping he would come in and climb into bed beside her. Though it had taken nearly ten of their fourteen years together to cultivate an overwhelming love for her husband, it had happened. She had hopes of their growing old together and being grandma and grandpa to Bethany's children. Now this had happened. Chuck had been accused of molesting his coworker. As much as she wanted to believe in his innocence, visions of him with that woman kept playing in her mind. If only he had never taken Michelle home that night, perhaps none of this would have ever happened.

Startled by a soft rap on the door, she grabbed the sheet and pulled it tightly about her neck.

"Can — can I come in?"

Though the voice was barely audible, she knew it was Chuck. "Sure. Come on in."

Still dressed in the shirt and trousers he had worn to work that day, he moved slowly into the room and headed toward the bathroom. "I forgot my toothbrush."

"Oh."

"Sorry to bother you."

"No bother."

He moved quickly into the bathroom, then came out carrying his toothbrush and a new tube of toothpaste. "Okay if I take this?" he asked, holding out the tube.

"You bought it."

"I think I've got everything else I need."

"There are extra blankets on the top shelf of the closet," Mindy told him as he stopped at the foot of the bed and stood gazing at her. "And clean towels and washcloths in the linen closet."

"I didn't do it, Mindy."

She closed her book and leaned back onto her pillow.

"Somehow I'm going to prove it to you."

"I hope so, Chuck — I really hope so. But it sounds like another one of those unprovable cases of 'he said — she said,' the kind so many of the sports figures have been involved in lately. Her word against his. How can you prove which person is telling the truth in cases like that?"

He grabbed hold of the bedpost, pressing his forehead against it. "I know, but believe me, this was not one of those consensual things. You have to have made contact with the person to have that kind of excuse or reason apply. I had no physical contact with that woman."

Mindy let out a loud sigh. "Seems one of this nation's high public officials made a statement similar to that, and the next day he recanted."

"That won't happen here. I can assure you nothing improper happened," he said firmly, giving her a slight glare. "I have nothing to recant."

"I — I hope that's true, Chuck —" She stopped, unable to speak what was in her heart.

"If our roles were reversed, I'd feel exactly the same way. Even the thought of another man touching you in a more than friendly way sickens me."

"That could never happen, Chuck. Even though our life together has been rocky, I would never cheat on you."

"Nor would I cheat on you! You have to believe that, Mindy. You have no idea how hard all of this is on me!"

He started for the door, stopping halfway across the room to turn back to her. "I'll set my alarm early like I said I would."

She gave him a faint smile. "Thank you. I'm sure you want to protect our daughter as much as I do."

"I am going to prove my innocence, Mindy. Just promise you'll give me some time. I don't know how I'll do it, but I'll find a way. I have to. I — I love you."

"I love you, too, Chuck. That's what makes this so difficult. If I didn't love you, it wouldn't matter, but I do love you. More than you'll ever know. I want you to prove your innocence so our marriage can continue, but —"

He held up his palm between them. "I will, Mindy. I have to."

She flipped over onto her side, turning her face away from him, knowing if she looked at his sad expression one more time, she would break out in tears. "Good night, Chuck. I do love you."

"Good night, Mindy. I love you, too."

A few seconds later she heard the door close softly, and she was alone in the king-sized bed, her tears dampening the pillow.

The strain was still there between them the next morning at the breakfast table, but for Bethany's sake Mindy worked hard at keeping things as normal as possible. And she could sense Chuck was doing the same. The child had suffered enough at their hands during the first ten years of her life, until they had figured out a way at least to appear compatible. But the funny thing was, once they decided to look as if they were trying to get along and live life as a normal family, they had actually begun to like each other. They had even felt some of the same vibes they'd experienced during the weeks they had dated and those first few months after their wedding. That was before Mindy discovered she was pregnant and Chuck lowered the boom on her by expecting her to quit the job she loved and be a twenty-four–seven, stay-at-home mom. Her pregnancy had come as a total shock, and though she had wanted someday to have children, she was not prepared to put her career on hold as Chuck expected her to. At least not until she had reached the top of her profession.

"Why do I have to be the one to give up my job and stay at home? What about you?" she had asked him, fully believing he was an equal partner in their marriage. "Why can't you put your job on hold and stay at home? I'm making more money than you are! We could far better afford to live on my salary than on your commissions."

He had countered by reminding her that God made women to be the child bearers, so He also must expect women to be the caregivers.

In anticipation of the birth of their first child, once they had both accepted the fact that a baby was on its way, and wanting to make sure the baby had a good start in life, Mindy had arranged to take a six-week leave of absence from Health Care Incorporated. She served there as assistant manager — a well-paying position she had worked long and hard to attain. She had known that with that promotion her earning potential would be unlimited, provided she would be available to travel to their many branch offices, spending as much time at each one as necessary. She had hoped that once her six weeks' leave was up, Chuck would change his mind, take over, and become a stay-at-home dad, but that was not to be. Though she resented his pigheaded, unchangeable attitude, she had to admit she loved each minute she spent with their new daughter, soon realizing that being away from her for long periods of time was nearly intolerable.

She glanced to see if Bethany was watching her and, finding her daughter engrossed with her bowl of hot oatmeal, eyed Chuck with a frown. He was dressed in a suit and tie, the way he normally dressed when going to the office. Why was he dressed like that?

As if reading her mind, Chuck took his last swig of coffee and rose to his feet, folding up the sports section of the morning paper and stuffing it under his arm. "See you ladies tonight," he said as cheerily as if nothing had happened and it was a normal day.

Where is he going?

"Got a full day ahead of me." He bent and kissed Bethany's cheek. "Have a good day at school, Princess."

"Bye, Daddy."

Stepping up close beside Mindy, Chuck hesitated only for a second before leaning over and kissing her on the forehead. "I'll call you later."

After Bethany left for school and Mindy finished cleaning up the kitchen, she slipped into her dress, checked her appearance in the mirror, then grabbed her briefcase. She was already in the hallway off the kitchen with her hand on the doorknob when the phone rang. After a quick glance at her watch, she rushed to answer it.

"Hi," a male voice said softly. "Is the coast clear?"

"Clear? If you mean is Bethany gone, the answer is yes. Her ride picked her up about ten minutes ago. Where are you, Chuck?"

"I'm at the service station. I — I thought it might be best if Bethany saw me leave for work as usual. I sure don't want to have to explain to her why I'm without a job."

"I was on my way out the door. What are your plans for today?"

"I — I thought I'd come back home. There's no place else for me to go. Somehow I'd like to prove my innocence, but how do you go about doing something like that? Like you said, it's my word against hers."

Mindy nervously twined the phone cord around her fingers. "Have you talked to Michelle about this?"

"No."

"Don't you think you should? If you are innocent, maybe you can talk some sense into her head — let her know what this is doing to your life."

"I've thought about it, but —"

"But what, Chuck? You can't sit idly by and do nothing. You have to take action of some kind."

"I don't want to talk to her in private, not after the kind of accusations she's made, and I don't want to talk to her at the office with everyone listening in on our conversation. I'm furious with her for what she did. I'm not sure I could talk to her face-to-face without losing my temper."

"So? Are you just going to let things ride?"

No answer came.

"Chuck, did you hear me? Are you still there?"

"I — I'm here. I just don't know what to do. Can I meet you for lunch?"

She pulled the phone from her ear and stared into it. *Have lunch?* "I — I don't know."

"Look, sweetie — I can't blame you for reacting the way you are. The whole thing is ridiculous. I can only imagine what it's doing to you, but I — I need you, Mindy. I can't stand this wedge between us. It's miserable in that guest room knowing you're sleeping all alone just a few yards from me. I wanted so much to hold you in my arms and kiss your sweet face. I barely slept a wink last night."

"I had a hard time sleeping, too." She pinched the bridge of her nose between her thumb and her forefinger. "Okay, I'll meet you for lunch, but not at a restaurant. I'll meet you at home and fix us a bowl of soup."

"Thanks, Mindy. You have no idea how much I need you to help me get through this. And don't worry about fixing the soup. I have all the time in the world to do it. I'll open a can of something and have it hot when you get there."

"See you at noon." Staring off into space, she hung up the phone. She loved Chuck. Though they'd had their troubles, she'd never once thought about him cheating on her. With a lump in her throat, she picked up her briefcase and headed out the door. *What is it they say? The wife is the last to know?*

When she reentered the house on Victor Lane at five minutes past twelve, the enticing aroma of tomato soup greeted her, and she had to smile. For years Chuck had resisted her urgings to keep canned soup in their pantry, reminding her that his mother always made their soups from scratch. She had reminded him that was his mother's choice. Not hers. Mindy was a good cook and spent many hours in the kitchen preparing the things he and Bethany liked, but homemade tomato soup didn't happen to be one of them, any more than his mother would prepare a homemade quiche as Mindy did, which happened to be one of Chuck's favorites. After many an argument Chuck had finally conceded that prepared and fast foods had their place in busy lives.

"Soup's hot, and the table is set," he said, meeting her at the door, taking her jacket from her hands. "How'd your morning go?"

"Okay. I guess." She felt a small smile quirk at her lips as she washed her hands at the sink before sliding into her chair. Wasn't that what June Cleaver always asked Ward Cleaver when he came home from the office? All Chuck needed was an apron tied around his waist, high heels, and a string of pearls.

"I've been thinking about what you said.

I'm going to call Michelle and ask her to meet me someplace so we can talk about this." He gave her a shy grin. "Would — would you come with me? I don't want to be alone with her."

She folded her hands on the table and eyed him suspiciously. "You want me to go with you? Isn't it a bit unorthodox to have the little woman go along with the accused man?"

He reached across the table and cupped his hand over hers. "I — I need you there, Mindy. That's why I wanted you to have lunch with me. I want you to hear the entire story before we talk to her."

Her heart sank. "Entire story? You mean there really is more?"

"Everything I've said is true. I — I just haven't told you all of it."

The room began to swirl, making her dizzy. Though Mindy had never fainted in her life, she was sure this was going to be the first time. "Oh, Chuck, I'm not sure I'm up to this."

"Don't worry, sweetheart. I meant it when I said nothing was going on between that woman and me. I think you'll better understand if you hear me out."

She pulled her hands from his and linked

them in her lap, her heart doing the fifty-yard dash. "I'm listening."

CHAPTER THREE

Chuck rose and walked to the refrigerator. Then, taking out a carton of milk and pouring himself a glass, he returned it to the shelf and closed the door. "What I'm about to tell you is the whole story. As I told you yesterday, I did go to the diner with Michelle, and being a gentleman, I paid for our dinner."

"But that wasn't the end of it?" she asked with trepidation, almost dreading to hear his answer.

Chuck sat down at the table and hung his head. "No, it wasn't. When I got to my car the next evening, she was standing there waiting for me. She said she felt bad because she'd let me pay for our dinner and wanted me to go with her to try out a new pizza parlor in her neighborhood. You were still gone, and I didn't see any harm in it, so I went with her. It was all perfectly innocent."

Mindy nibbled on her lower lip. "On your

part maybe, but I'll bet not hers."

"Remember you called that night, and I told you I'd tried a new pizza place? I just didn't tell you I'd gone with Michelle."

Mindy gasped! Of course she remembered that night. She had been surprised Chuck would go alone to try out a new place. She had even kidded him about it, playfully asking him who had gone with him.

"Well, the next day was Saturday. I was messing around with that loose board on the porch floor you'd been wanting me to fix when the phone rang. It was Michelle, and she was crying. She said someone had tried to get into her apartment during the night and she was terrified. She hadn't lived there long and hadn't had a chance to get someone to put a dead bolt on her door. She begged me to come over and put one on. Even offered to pay me for it. Since it was a weekend, none of the places she'd called had anyone on staff to do it. She sounded so pitiful that I agreed. I took that dead bolt I'd purchased to put on our garage door, grabbed up my toolbox, and rushed right over. It didn't take me fifteen minutes to do the job. She thanked me, then offered me a cup of coffee and a piece of her homemade cheesecake. We had a nice visit. She asked all kinds of questions about you and Bethany, and since I like talking about the two of you, I answered them."

"How long did you stay?" Mindy prodded.

"Probably forty-five minutes. No more than an hour — then I left."

"Then what happened?"

"She called Sunday morning to thank me for putting the dead bolt on and said she'd slept soundly because of it. At the time I thought that was nice of her to call. Everyone likes to be appreciated for what they do."

His comment somewhat irked her. "Are you saying I don't let you know you're appreciated?"

He shook his head. "No! That's not what I meant at all. You're very good about thanking me for the things I do for you."

Feeling bad for responding without thinking first, she settled down and forced her tense face to relax. "There's more, isn't there?"

He fingered the salt and pepper shakers on the table without meeting her eyes. "The next weekend you had that meeting in Providence, and Bethany went to stay overnight with a girlfriend. I guess I'd mentioned to one of the guys at the office that I was going to be batching it for a day or two. Anyway, Michelle was waiting for me in the garage again that night. This time she held up two tickets to a Patriots game, telling me she'd heard me say I wanted to go and couldn't get tickets. So she'd called someone she knew whose brother worked in the Patriots' office and arranged with him to get the tickets for her. She said she wanted to take me as a thank-you for putting the dead bolt on her door."

"She sure knew which one of your buttons to push. I'll bet you jumped at the chance."

"Not at first. But I admit I did want to go. I offered to buy them from her, with the idea of taking one of the guys from work, but she wouldn't hear of it. She said she'd gone to a lot of work to get those tickets, that she, too, loved the Patriots, and it was her way of thanking me."

Mindy gave him an indignant stare. "So being the dedicated Patriots football fan that you are, you accepted."

"I tried to say no."

"But she kept at you until you said yes?"

"I didn't realize it at the time, since I really wanted to go to that game, but, yes, I guess she did." Chuck stood, wadded up his paper napkin, and tossed it into the wastebasket as he headed for the family room.

41

She followed him and seated herself opposite him, folding her hands in her lap. "So you drove her to Foxboro?"

"Hey, it wasn't that far! The Gillette stadium in Foxboro may be in Massachusetts, but it's still only a forty-five-minute drive from here."

Mindy rolled her eyes. "A lot can happen in forty-five minutes. Not to mention the return time."

Chuck gave her a disgruntled look. "We barely talked on the way over there. Most of the time we listened to the pregame show on the radio. And during the game it was so noisy you couldn't talk if you wanted to."

"Did you give her high fives when the Patriots scored, the way you do me when we go to the games?"

"Yeah, but I give high fives to everyone sitting around us — you know that."

"Sometimes you even hug me when they score. Did you hug her?"

With an air of indignation, Chuck leaned back against the sofa and crossed his arms over his chest. "Of course not! What do you take me for?"

"I'm more concerned with what she took you for," she answered coolly.

She could tell her inference upset him,

but he did not comment. He just stared at her.

"You want me to continue with my story?" he finally asked in a low, controlled voice.

She could almost see his teeth gritting. "Yes, go on."

"This isn't easy, but I want you to know everything. Okay?"

She nodded. "I'm sure it isn't easy."

He rose slowly, stuffing his hands into his pockets as he moved to the window and stared out into the backyard. "The game was great. The Patriots won. We listened to the coach's postgame interview on the way back home. We got to her apartment, and I was letting her off at the front door before heading on home when she said she'd baked a new cake recipe and wanted me to come up and try it out."

"Come up and see my etchings? That's an old line. Surely you didn't fall for it," Mindy said sarcastically.

"I almost did. I was so excited about their win that I felt like celebrating, and you weren't here to celebrate with me. I thought about it but didn't go. If it had been Jake, it would have been a different story."

"It wasn't Jake, though," Mindy pointed out.

"No, it wasn't." Chuck let out his breath.

"What I meant as a friendly gesture, she must have taken another way."

Both Mindy and Chuck turned as the kitchen door opened and Bethany appeared, her face flushed and her hair askew.

CHAPTER FOUR

"I think I'm getting the flu. The school nurse said I had a temperature. I told her both of you were at work, so since she was going to pick up her lunch at the drive-thru down on the corner, she brought me home. What are you doing here? You guys never eat lunch at home."

Mindy flashed a worried glance toward her husband, then turned her attention back to Bethany, her mind racing for a good excuse, one her daughter would believe.

"It was a spur-of-the-moment idea. We were both hungry for soup." Chuck reached out and placed his palm on Bethany's forehead. "You do feel a bit warm."

"Have you had lunch yet?" Mindy hurried to the range and checked the soup pan. "There's a little tomato soup left."

Bethany squiggled up her face and spread her hand across her abdomen. "I — I don't want anything to eat. My tummy doesn't feel so good. The nurse said there's a bunch of that twenty-four-hour stuff going around. I guess I got it."

Chuck hurried to his daughter and, after taking her book bag from her hands, helped pull off her coat. "I'll check the medicine cabinet. I think we still have some of those tablets the doctor recommended when you had that bout with the flu last year."

Mindy wrapped her arm around her daughter's slim shoulders. "Why don't you get into your pajamas, sweetie, and try to take a nap? Do you feel like drinking a cup of hot tea?"

Bethany winced as her hand covered her mouth. "Hot tea? Yuck! I hate hot tea."

"Then how about some spritzy-type soda pop? Sometimes that'll help settle your stomach."

"I might try to drink a little bit, but not the hot tea."

Bethany was already crawling into her pajamas when Mindy took a glass of soda into her room. "Try to drink this. Your body needs fluids."

"Drink some when you take this tablet," Chuck said, coming into the room. "Do you want me to call the doctor?"

"No, Daddy. I'm not a baby. It's just the plain old flu. It's not that serious. A bunch of the kids at school have had it, and only two of them have died so far."

Chuck's eyes widened. "Some of the kids died? I didn't hear about it! Was it on the news?"

Bethany let out a strained laugh. "Dad! It was a joke!"

Despite her concern for her daughter, Mindy had to laugh. Normally Chuck was the prankster.

He lifted his arms in surrender. "Okay, ladies, you got me!"

"Ohh!" Her face turning an ashen white, Bethany rushed past them into the bathroom, slamming the door behind her.

"I'll go to her," Mindy said, moving quickly across the room.

Chuck hurried past her, beating her to the door. "No, I will. You have a soft stomach."

"But I'm her mother," she insisted, reaching for the doorknob.

"And I'm her father."

"I don't want either one of you," a small, weak voice responded through the door. "Just leave me alone. I'm — I'm about to —"

The two stood staring at each other, listening to the strange sounds coming through the locked door.

Eventually Bethany emerged, her face

pale, with damp curls resting on her forehead. "I — I feel better now."

Mindy slipped her hand beneath her daughter's elbow and lovingly helped her cross the room.

"Can I get you anything, Princess? More soda pop? Crackers?" Chuck asked, supporting her on the other side as they helped her into bed.

"No, Dad! Don't even mention food, please!"

"Do you need another blanket?" Mindy asked, tucking the quilt beneath her daughter's chin, feeling the need to do something to make Bethany feel better.

Bethany gave her head a slight shake. "Would you put a plastic bag in my wastebasket and set it by the side of the bed? My tummy still feels yucky."

"I'll get a bag," her father volunteered as he rushed out of the room.

"Mama?"

"Yes?"

"Are you mad at Daddy?"

Mindy quickly pasted on a smile. "Mad at Daddy? Whatever makes you ask such a thing?"

Bethany took on a solemn look. "I — I heard the two of you arguing last night. Like you used to argue when I was little. It — it scared me."

"Oh, honey, all parents argue once in a while. We're humans. We can't always agree on everything. I'll bet your friends' parents argue sometimes, too." It was the best answer she could come up with on the spur of the moment.

Bethany let out a sigh. "I know, and some of them have gotten divorces, too. I remember the many times you and Daddy talked about divorce when I was a little kid. I — I was afraid it was happening again."

Mindy sat down on the side of the bed and began to stroke Bethany's clammy forehead. "Your dad and I always worked things out, didn't we?"

Bethany gave a slight nod.

"I'll be honest with you, sweetheart. Those first ten years were hard for both of us. We were each pretty selfish, and neither wanted to give in to the other. If we hadn't had you and experienced the joy you brought into our lives, we might have split up. But we didn't. We hung in there, and I can honestly say the past four years have been the happiest of my life. I guess your father and I finally grew up and began to act like adults."

"I — I wish you both loved God like I do."

Mindy gave her daughter's shoulder a patronizing pat. "We go to church with you now. Isn't that enough?"

Chuck came back into the room with the plastic bag. "Isn't what enough?" He gave the bag a flip to open it, then picked up the wastebasket.

"I was telling Mom I wished the two of you loved God like I do."

He gave her a puzzled look as he placed the bag in the little basket. "We go to church with you nearly every Sunday."

"That's what I was telling her," Mindy added, suddenly becoming her husband's ally.

"I — I told Mom I heard the two of you arguing last night."

Chuck flashed a glance toward his wife.

"I explained we were just having a slight disagreement." Mindy kept up her fake smile. "Nothing for her to worry about."

Bethany's eyes filled with tears. "I — I don't know what I'd do if you guys got a divorce like some of my friends' parents have. You have to promise me you'll never let that happen."

Mindy's heart sank. How could she make a promise like that in light of what was going on? If she ever discovered Chuck had been unfaithful to her and that woman's accusations were true, she could never live another night under the same roof with him.

Not even for Bethany's sake. *Am I being honest with myself? If Bethany begged me to stay in our marriage, would I still leave?*

Chuck reached out and took Mindy's hand, his thumb stroking her knuckles. "I don't want that ever to happen either, Princess. I love your mother and can't imagine life without her."

Mindy wanted to burst into tears at his words, her heart soaring up and down on an emotional roller-coaster ride. She did not want a divorce either, but if —

"Mom? You'd never divorce Daddy, would you?" Bethany's pleading eyes pierced straight to her mother's heart.

Pulling free of Chuck's grasp, Mindy rose quickly and grinned at her child. "You need to put this silly kind of talk out of your mind, young lady, and concentrate on taking a nap. Sleep is the best thing for your body right now."

"You're not going to go back to work and leave me, are you? What if I have to throw up again?"

Chuck leaned over Bethany and kissed her forehead. "I'll be here all afternoon. I have some things in my briefcase I can work on. I'll check on you again soon, but call if you need me. I'll be in the family room."

Liar! Mindy had to bite her tongue to keep

from reminding Chuck he had no job to go to and certainly no work in his briefcase. "Since your father will be here," she said, trying to keep her hurt feelings under control, "I'm going back to my office. But if you want me to come home, just give me a call, and I'll be here immediately. And, Bethany, stay off that computer. You've been spending entirely too much time on it lately. What you need is bed rest. Okay?"

The two of them backed out of the door, closing it gently behind them.

"Work in your briefcase?" Mindy asked sarcastically in an exaggerated whisper once they were alone in the family room and, she hoped, out of earshot.

Chuck sat down on the sofa, his head in his hands. "You didn't want me to tell her the real reason I'm home, did you?"

She tugged her coat on and picked up her purse from the coffee table, slinging the strap over her shoulder. "Of course not. You heard what she said in there."

"I never thought she'd hear us last night. I assumed she was asleep."

"Do you have any idea what this would do to her if she found out?"

Chuck lifted his face slowly. "The truth will prove my innocence, Mindy."

She put a finger to her lips. "Shh. She may

be listening."

"But I never got to finish. I need to tell you the rest of the story."

She gave her head a shake. "Not now. It'll have to wait until we're sure she can't hear us. I'm going to the office. Call if you need me."

He gave a slight shrug, stood, and followed her to the door. "I love you, Mindy."

She turned the knob and stepped onto the porch. "I love you, too, Chuck. More than you know."

"Michelle's accusations aren't true, sweetheart."

She turned and stared at him for a moment, scanning his face for any telltale expression. "I hope not, Chuck, for all our sakes."

Mindy crawled into her car and headed down the street toward her office, but on a sudden whim she turned the steering wheel in the opposite direction.

Chuck watched until Mindy's car was out of sight. He loved that woman more than life itself, though those first ten years of their married life had been a love-hate battle almost every day. Mindy had done so many things that irritated him that he'd found it difficult to live with her. Being a neat freak and raised by a mother who was one, his creed had always been to put things away the minute you were finished with them. Toothpaste. Toothbrush. Hang your coat in the closet. Sort your clothing out by type and color when you place it on the closet rod. Suits together. Trousers together. Jackets together. Shirts together — sorted by whites, blues, greens, and so on, starched just the way he liked them. Underwear and T-shirts sorted and folded in the same exact rectangular shapes and piled neatly in the drawers. On and on and on, but everything had been precise and in order, with a place for everything and everything in its place. Both the interior and the exterior of his car were always sparkling clean and devoid of trash. He had never been late to an activity or business appointment in his life, always preferring to arrive early. He retired early and rose early, selecting his next day's attire before going to bed. His life had been thoroughly organized and virtually stress free.

Until he met Mindy.

The pretty little blue-eyed blond with the cute dimples, a button nose, and Southern twang in her voice made him forget everything. It didn't bother him at all that Mindy was the opposite of him, that she was late for every date, making him wait as much as a half hour for her to finish applying her makeup and get dressed. He didn't mind that she left fast-food wrappers in his car, spilled soft drinks on his floor mats, left her apartment in disarray with clothing and shoes strewn everywhere, dirty dishes piled on the kitchen counter, magazines scattered on the tables and floor — leaving it to look as if a tornado had just roared through. Even the fresh bouquets of flowers he brought her remained in their vases for days after they had wilted and lost their fragrance. As long as Mindy was by his side and he could claim her as his girlfriend, none of those things mattered. All that mattered was that they were together.

But all that changed after the wedding and the two of them took up residence in Chuck's apartment, which was considerably larger than hers.

"But, Chuck," he remembered her saying when he'd suggested she take time to organize her belongings, "I simply don't have the time." Then she'd spend hours talking on the phone to her girlfriends about ridiculous things that didn't count, reading those dumb fashion magazines or giving herself a manicure and a pedicure, trying out a dozen colors of polish until she could decide on the right one, the other eleven bottles sitting on the bathroom counter, their lids off, just waiting to be spilled. The laundry never got done unless he did it, and Mindy did not even know where the dry cleaner's shop was located. Even the grocery shopping and most of the cooking were left up to him, though they ate out most of the time because Mindy preferred it. That was the way it was at her house when she was growing up. It was good enough for her mother, and it was good enough for her.

If that was not bad enough, since Mindy hadn't been his mother's first choice for a daughter-in-law, his mother was constantly at him, reminding him he knew what Mindy was like before he married her.

"Daddy."

He startled at the sound of his daughter's voice calling from her bedroom. "Can you bring another clean bag for the wastebasket? I don't feel so good."

Mindy sucked in a breath of air, squared her shoulders, and pushed open the door to Cox Machine and Parts Company.

"Hello, Mrs. O'Connor." The reception-ist's eyes rounded as if she was surprised to see Mindy standing there. "Chuck — Chuck isn't here," the woman said, looking embarrassed.

"I know. I'm here to see Clarisse. Is she in?" Mindy asked, trying to act nonchalant, as if everything were fine in the O'Connor household.

"I'll buzz her and tell her you're here." The receptionist gave her a questioning frown, then spoke into her headset to Clarisse. "She said to come on back. You know where her office is, don't you?"

Mindy nodded and headed toward the elevator. She punched three, waited impatiently until the elevator ground its way to the third floor, then stepped out smiling, hoping her face wouldn't reflect the turmoil she felt inside. Clarisse was standing at the door of her office. She motioned her in, closing the door behind her.

"I — I didn't expect to see you here today," she said awkwardly, pointing to a chair and seating herself behind her big desk.

"I have to talk to you." Mindy worked hard at keeping the nervousness from her voice, but it came through anyway. "I — I need some answers, and I'm not sure who can give them to me. I thought maybe you could help."

"You know I'll do anything I can. I'm sick

about Chuck's suspension," the woman answered kindly, her face showing sincere concern. "What do you want to know?"

"I assume you've heard the accusations that woman made against him."

"Unfortunately, yes. We've all heard them."

Mindy felt as awkward as a pig on ice skates. "Do — do you believe her?"

"Absolutely not! I didn't like that woman from the start. Had bad vibes about her. From her employment record she doesn't stay anyplace very long. I wish she'd never come here."

Those words were like a soothing salve on Mindy's troubled soul, and she began to cry. "Oh, Clarisse, you have no idea how much it means to me to hear you say that. I–I've wanted to believe Chuck, but —"

"I'd have a hard time believing my husband if someone accused him the way Michelle accused Chuck. You have every right to be angry about this, but please give your husband the benefit of the doubt until you hear otherwise. Chuck's a good guy."

Clarisse pulled a box of tissues from a drawer and pushed it across her desk. Mindy took one and dabbed at her eyes. "I — I don't know the woman. I'm not even sure if I've ever seen her."

"She's not a bad looker, but nothing special. Most of the women in the office dislike her and have from the start. She gets along fine with the men, but the women — ?" Clarisse raised her hand and gave a flip of her wrist. "None of us like her. Did you ever get the feeling when you met someone that they couldn't be trusted?"

"Not really."

"I hadn't either until the day I met Michelle, but I felt it then."

Mindy looked up and frowned. "Really? Why? Was it something she said or did?"

Clarisse leaned forward in her chair and linked her fingers together, resting her hands on her desk. "No, just a feeling. She's one of those loners — you know what I mean? Most of us women congregate in the employees' lounge for breaks, drinking coffee or soft drinks, laughing and talking together about the boss, our jobs, our families. Not that one. She stays pretty much to herself or off talking to the men. The rest of us haven't really gotten to know her, and she's been here for nearly six months now."

"Does she dress provocatively?"

"Provocatively?" Clarisse gave her head a firm shake. "No, just the opposite. She dresses very businesslike. Like the proverbial wolf in sheep's clothing, if you ask me."

"I probably shouldn't put you on the spot and ask," Mindy said, lowering her eyes and twisting the tissue between her fingers, "but have you ever seen anything improper going on between Chuck and her? Like a wink or a look that didn't seem right to you?"

"Not a one — from Chuck to her. But I can't say I haven't seen the reverse. I'd say she's had her eye on him from day one."

Mindy's heart sank. This was not what she wanted to hear.

"But Chuck?" the woman continued. "I doubt he ever noticed. All he ever talks about is you. That man is crazy in love with you."

Mindy felt herself blushing. "Clarisse, you've known us for what? Ten years? You know how troubled our marriage was until four years ago. I think Chuck and I honestly loved each other those first ten years, but we sure weren't in sync. We couldn't seem to see eye to eye on anything, from how the house should be kept, to the foods we ate, to when we should have a baby, to who should stay at home and care for her, to everything else that pertained to our lives."

Clarisse gave her a placating smile. "Don't they say opposites attract? Apparently it was true with the two of you. But you worked it out. You're to be commended for that. I've never seen a happier married couple than the two of you these past few years. I don't know if you went to a marriage counselor or what, but I know I've seen a real change in both of you."

"I hate to admit it, Clarisse, but I think we both grew up. We finally realized what our arguments and battles were doing to our family. Poor little Bethany was always in the middle." Mindy smiled through her tears. "Did you ever see that movie about the little girl who decided to divorce her parents?"

Clarisse nodded. "Yeah, I saw it. My husband and I watched it again not long ago on TV."

"That's what happened to us on Bethany's ninth birthday. She watched it on TV at a friend's house. The next morning she came into the kitchen with her little suitcase and asked Chuck for five hundred dollars. She said she was tired of all our arguing and had decided to divorce us. She wanted the five hundred dollars to pay a lawyer to draw up the papers. Chuck, thinking it was a joke, asked her where she planned to live." Mindy paused, the scene playing out in her head. That scene had changed their lives.

Clarisse let out a gasp. "She was serious?"

Mindy nodded, remembering the determination on her daughter's face. "She said she didn't know where she'd live, but any place, even jail, would be better than living with us."

Clarisse leaned back in her chair, her hand covering her heart. "Oh my. That must have upset both of you."

"It did. We knew she didn't like to hear us argue, but we never realized how deeply it affected her until that day."

"What did you do?"

"I remember it like it was yesterday. We threw our arms around Bethany and each other and vowed we would change. And we did. Although we continued to annoy each other with our habits, we kept our complaints to ourselves, and you know what? It wasn't long before we each barely noticed the faults in the other, and we both certainly enjoyed the newfound peace and quiet. We noticed an instant change in Bethany, too. Where she had been an extremely quiet, moody child, she blossomed, a smile constantly on her face. Her teachers noticed it, too, and asked us what had happened to cause such a transformation."

Clarisse clapped her hands together. "That's wonderful! I hadn't realized what had happened, but I noticed a change in

Chuck, too. Oh, he's always been a born salesman, and everyone likes him, but there was something about his countenance, a glow, a feeling of self-pride that began to show on his face." She gave Mindy a grin. "Up to that time he talked constantly about Bethany, but he rarely said a word about you. After that, though, he talked about you constantly, saying how happy he was being married to you and what a wonderful wife and mother you were."

"He actually said that about me?"

"Many times. Too numerous to count."

"I — I didn't know."

"That's why it shocked all of us when Michelle made her accusations. It wasn't like the Chuck we all knew and loved, to behave like that. Especially with a woman like her, when he had such a beautiful wife at home."

"But you never saw Chuck do anything improper?"

"Never. Even when Dixie told us what she'd heard in the rest—"

"Dixie told you about that phone call?"

Clarisse nodded. "Dixie is a nice person, but she couldn't keep her mouth shut if her life depended on it."

"I — I don't know what to do, Clarisse," Mindy confided, knowing Clarisse could be trusted. "How do you prove someone's innocence when it's their word against the other person's? I'm beginning to understand how those star athletes feel when a charge like this is made against them. As Chuck said, it's one person's word against the other's, with no witnesses to prove one way or the other."

Clarisse shook her head. "Many a person's reputation has probably been ruined for life for that very reason."

Mindy stared at her hands for a moment, then lifted her eyes to meet Clarisse's. "I have to know the truth. For everyone's sake."

"Know what I'd do if I were in your shoes?" Clarisse asked, her question surprising Mindy. "I'd stalk that woman. I'd watch her every move, even go Dumpster-diving."

Mindy frowned. "Dumpster-diving? What's that?"

"You know, go through the trash she throws away. I heard a trash collector interviewed on TV once on one of those investigative shows. He said he could tell you almost anything you wanted to know about a person just by looking through their trash."

A giggle escaped Mindy's lips. "Dumpster-diving, huh? I may give it a try."

"I figure this isn't the first time she's done

something like this, and it won't be the last. I'd talk to the people she worked with before she came here. Maybe talk to her neighbors to see if she makes a habit of inviting men to her apartment. I'd —"

"You'd do all of that?"

Clarisse narrowed her eyes and leaned forward again, anchoring her elbows on her desk. "You bet I would! Why not? What do you have to lose? If I loved my husband the way I know you love Chuck, I wouldn't leave a stone or, in this case, a trash can un-turned until I learned the truth. Even if it hurt, I'd have to know what happened and who the guilty party was."

Mindy stared at the woman. She'd never seen her this intense. "I — I wouldn't know where to start. I don't even know where she lives."

Clarisse let a small, mischievous smile curl at her lips. "I know. I have most of that information right here on my computer. All I have to do is punch a few keys on the keyboard."

"But isn't that information confidential?"

"Oh, I didn't say I was going to give it to you." Clarisse tapped several keys and stared at the computer screen for a few seconds, then pulled a yellow steno pad from her top desk drawer, placed a pen on top of it, and, rising from her chair, shoved them both toward Mindy. "But if I just happen to have that information on my screen, and I just happen to go down the hall to the lunchroom to get us a cup of coffee, and you just happen to copy that information on this pad while I'm gone, is that my fault? Have I actually given it to you? Of course not. I wasn't even in the room." She gave Mindy a wink, then made her way out of her office, closing the door behind her.

Mindy's heart pounded so loudly she thought she could hear the sound echoing off the walls of the little office. She circled the desk, sat in Clarisse's chair, and quickly began to copy the information onto the pad. Armed with almost everything she needed to find out more about the elusive Michelle, she nervously pulled the sheets off the pad, folded them, and put them into her purse.

Within minutes the office door opened and Clarisse was back, carrying two cups of steaming hot coffee. With a glance toward the computer screen, the woman lifted her brows, her lips forming a slow smile. "Oh? Did I leave that computer turned on? How careless of me."

After enjoying the hot coffee, which helped to calm her frazzled nerves, Mindy thanked Clarisse, said her good-byes, and moved out the door, heading back toward the elevator. When it arrived, she stepped in and pressed the button marked LOBBY. As the doors began to close, a woman's voice called out, "Hold it, please!"

Instinctively Mindy stuck her arm through the opening, and the door reversed its direction and opened wide as a woman dressed in a beige pantsuit hurried inside, her arms filled with file folders, a pencil stuck over her ear. Though neither woman said anything, Mindy felt the woman's gaze on her, and it made her uncomfortable. *Could this be Michelle?* When they reached the first floor, she waited until the woman was out then stepped out and hurried to her car, clutching the information she needed to do a search on her husband's accuser.

It was nearly six thirty before Mindy finished loading the dinner dishes into the dishwasher. She went into the living room and, trying to appear as casual as possible, moved up to Chuck's chair, hoping the game show he was watching would keep his attention and he wouldn't ask her any questions. "I'm going to go pick up some more toothpaste and a couple of rolls of paper towels. I should be back in an hour or so. Bethany is in her room."

Chuck barely glanced her way. "Could you

get me some deodorant while you're there?"

Mindy winced. She had not planned on stopping at a store. Now she would have to if she wanted to cover her tracks. "Sure. Usual kind?"

"Yeah," he answered with a deep sigh, his eyes still fixed on the screen. "You know the kind."

Relieved he did not suggest going with her, Mindy hurriedly snatched up her purse and jacket and headed toward the door.

After rushing into the store and picking up the few items she had mentioned to Chuck, as well as his deodorant, she drove to the address she'd scribbled on the sheet that lay folded in her purse. She'd had no need to check the address; it was etched into her memory.

The neighborhood was much more upscale than she'd expected it would be, filled with lovely townhouses and twin homes. How could a single woman who worked as a secretary afford such nice housing? Maybe she had a roommate to share expenses.

Since the porch light was lit, she easily located the proper address — a two-story, red-brick townhouse done in a colonial style, with black shutters and white trim. Slowly she pulled to a stop across the street and turned off the lights and engine, her heart beating wildly within her chest. *Think, Mindy! You've watched movies with stakeouts before. What did they do? Maybe you should have brought your binoculars.*

This is ridiculous! She stiffened in her seat with a mocking shake of her head. *I feel like an idiot. What did I expect to find? It was a dumb idea to come here.*

She fingered the key in the ignition, intending to get out of there and never come back, when the front door of the townhouse opened and a woman stepped out onto the porch. *Michelle! The woman in the elevator. No wonder she gave me the eye!*

Instinctively Mindy scrunched down in the seat, lowering her head, while at the same time trying to peek through the upper opening in her steering wheel. Other than the few seconds she'd had to observe Michelle at the office, she had never seen the woman before; but considering she was the one causing a rift in her family, Mindy knew she would never forget that face.

She narrowed her eyes into a squint, trying for a better look at the woman. *What is she doing, standing on the porch that way? Why doesn't she either leave or go back inside?* Still peering through the odd-shaped slot in the steering wheel and suddenly realizing how irrationally she was behaving, Mindy uttered a small laugh. *What's the matter with me? I'm being paranoid. It's dark outside. She can't see me!* Relaxing a bit, she straightened and leaned back against the seat, circling her arms about the steering wheel, her eyes once again focused on her rival.

Rival? The word struck horror in her heart! *Is that what that woman is? My rival? For what? My husband's affections? His dedication? His respect?*

So caught up was she in pondering the answers to her questions, she barely noticed the red Mercedes as it pulled into the townhouse driveway and stopped. Michelle closed the door, hurried down the few steps, and crawled into the passenger's side. Though the light from the porch lamp was dim, Mindy could tell the woman was dressed in an attractive beige coat and very high heels and had her hair swept up in a French twist. All sorts of scenarios raced through her mind. Maybe Michelle was having dinner with an old friend. Or perhaps a group of women. Or maybe, just maybe, a man. A man she had made a play for, as she had done with Chuck? Could another unsuspecting wife be sitting at home somewhere in Warren, Rhode Island, unaware

Michelle had given up on Chuck and was now after her husband? A shudder coursed through Mindy's body at the thought. *Oh, Chuck, please don't be lying to me!*

As soon as the Mercedes was out of sight, Mindy started her car and drove off, no closer to having answers than when she had come, and feeling very much alone.

The house was quiet when she entered. No doubt Bethany had gone to bed. She slipped out of her coat, hung it in the front closet, and made her way through the darkened family room toward the kitchen, half-hoping, since it appeared the TV was turned off, her husband had retired, too.

"I was beginning to get worried. You've been gone a long time."

Whirling around quickly, she found Chuck sitting in his recliner in the darkness. "I — I" — she fumbled for words, knowing she'd have to cover for herself with a lie — "I ran into a friend at the supermarket, and we got to talking. You know how that is. Time gets away from you." Hoping for a nonconfrontational change of subject, she asked, "Bethany go on to bed?"

Chuck clicked on the lamp beside his chair, bathing the room in light. "Yeah, about a half hour ago. She must be feeling better. She was on the computer talking to one of her friends on that instant-message thing when I went into her room. She said to tell you good night."

"I really don't like her spending so much time on that computer." Mindy faked a yawn. "I'm going to get a glass of water, then turn in, too. Been a long day."

Chuck rose and, walking toward her, closed the gap between them. "I hate sleeping in the guest room."

His expression reminded her of a little boy whose mother had made him sit in a corner until he learned to behave properly. "I don't like sleeping alone either, Chuck, but I think it'd be best until this thing is settled and you've been exonerated."

"But I love you, Mindy. I thought you loved me!"

"I do love you, Chuck! That's why I'm so upset about this whole thing! That's why it hurts!"

He gave his head a frustrated shake. "It hurts me, too! Can't you see that? I'm caught in the middle, and I don't know how to convince you there is not, and never has been, anything going on between me and that woman."

Though she longed to throw herself into his arms, Mindy backed away, holding her palms up between them like a shield. "Then prove it, Chuck. Prove that woman is lying."

Chuck started to say something but turned his head aside and kept his silence. He shrugged, then moved past her toward the bedroom wing of the house, pausing long enough to say a simple "Good night" before making his way down the hall.

She listened until she heard the *click* of the guest room door, then, brushing a tear from her eye, walked into the kitchen for her drink of water.

Dressed in his maroon and navy blue plaid pajamas, the ones he wore only when they entertained overnight company or went on an occasional vacation, Chuck sat down on the edge of the bed and lowered his head into his hands. Never had he felt so rejected.

"Daddy? What are you doing in here?"

He turned quickly to find his sleepy-eyed daughter standing in the doorway. "Hi, Princess. I thought you were asleep," he answered sheepishly, not sure what else to say.

"I was, but I heard you and Mom talking. I wanted to ask her if she'd pack my lunch tomorrow. Thursday is pigs-in-a-blanket day in the school cafeteria. I hate the school's pigs-in-a-blanket! No one fixes them like

Mom does. I'd rather have a peanut butter and lettuce sandwich."

"Want me to ask her for you?" He moved toward the door. "I came in here to — to get a — ah — an old shirt I keep in the guest room closet. I was about to go back to our bedroom. Your mom is already there." The last thing he wanted was for Bethany to find him sleeping in the guest room.

Bethany nodded, then rubbed at her eyes with a yawn. "Sure. Thanks, Daddy."

Relieved, he watched her go, then hurried to their bedroom to convey her message. Mindy was standing in front of the mirror brushing her hair, wearing the yellow satin nightgown he had given her for her birthday. To Chuck she was a vision of loveliness. The years had been good to her. She was even more beautiful than she had been the day they'd eloped.

"Bethany wants you to fix her a sack lunch tomorrow," he told her, cautiously entering the room. "Guess she doesn't like the school's menu." To his surprise Mindy offered him a pleasant half-smile.

"Must be pigs-in-a-blanket day."

He nodded. "You know our daughter well."

"Very well." She placed the brush in a dresser drawer and turned to face him. "I may not have been the best of mothers her first few years, but I'm trying to make up for it."

"You're a good mother, Mindy. The best. Bethany is lucky to have you."

She moved to their bed and pulled back the lovely handmade Jacob's Ladder quilt Chuck had inherited from his grandmother. "I've always thought she was lucky to have you. You've been a terrific father to our daughter, but now —"

"Now you're not so sure?"

"That wasn't exactly what I was going to say." She picked up the pillow from her side of the bed and gave it two hard jabs with her fist to plump it up.

"But you were thinking it, right?"

Mindy slipped off her scuffies and slid between the sheets, pulling the covers up over her. "Chuck, it's late. Please let's not get into another discussion."

He moved to stand beside her, his arms dangling limply by his sides. "I don't want to argue with you, sweetheart. I just want you to believe me — that's all."

Mindy stared at him for a few seconds, then reached up and turned out the lamp on her nightstand. "On the way to your room, try not to wake Bethany again, okay?"

He stood in the semidarkness of the room,

a shaft of moonlight creeping around the edges of the shade its only light, and let out a deep sigh that came from the uttermost part of his being. "Good night, Mindy."

For the next week, each day as Mindy drove home from her office, she managed to swing by Michelle's condo. It was as if the car would not allow her to go home until she had made the out-of-the-way detour. But each time either Michelle wasn't at home yet or she had gone out for the evening or she was simply inside doing whatever single women did when they were home alone, and Mindy never saw her.

"I'm going crazy!" Chuck told her on Friday evening when he came into the house and slammed down his briefcase.

Mindy gave him an impatient frown. "Good thing Bethany has play rehearsal tonight and wasn't here to hear that outburst! What's wrong?"

He pulled off his sports coat and tossed it onto the chair, then yanked his tie from about his neck. "I've been all over town applying for jobs, but do you think anyone will hire me? Not a chance! Not after I tell them I've been suspended indefinitely and the reason why. You'd think I had the plague!"

"I'm sorry, Chuck. I never realized it

would be so hard to find another job," Mindy told him. "But in some ways you can't blame them."

Chuck gave her a ferocious stare. "How many times do I have to tell you that woman is lying?"

"Chuck! I'm on your side!" Mindy shot back defensively. "She's made some very serious charges against you! Put yourself in their place."

He grabbed her arms and leaned into her face. "Why should I expect anyone to believe those things didn't happen when my own wife, the woman who should know me best, doesn't believe me?"

His words went right to her gut. Mindy crossed to the sofa and sat down, moved by his obvious pain. "I want to believe you, Chuck," she said in a hushed, controlled voice. "I really do, and I'm trying to believe you, but as yet, other than simply denying the charge, you haven't given me any reason to believe you. Help me here. Give me some hope. So far you've given me nothing but a few denials. I need more. Surely you can understand that."

Chuck sat down beside her, wringing his hands, a deep scowl etched on his face. "I'm sorry, Mindy. I have no right to take my rage out on you, but I'm at my wit's end. I had a talk with Jake today, and although he is sympathetic, he says he has no choice but to keep me on suspension until I find a way to prove my innocence. Michelle is still working at her job, drawing her pay, with probably everyone feeling sorry for her. Meantime I can't even support my family."

Mindy could not resist the urge to place a comforting hand on his shoulder. "It's not as if we're destitute, Chuck. I'm still making good money. We have a sizable savings account and a couple of CDs, and our home is paid for. We have much to be thankful for."

He reached up and capped her hand with his long fingers. "I am thankful for those things, sweetheart, but you don't know what all this is doing to me. Though you make more money than I do, I still feel it's my responsibility as the husband and father of this family to provide for you and Bethany. How can I do that if I can't get a job?"

Mindy tugged her hand away. He made it all sound so hopeless. "I don't know, Chuck. I wish I did." How much longer could this go on? Chuck had become a different man from the one she had known all these years. He'd nearly given up on finding employment and had become the proverbial couch potato, a constant daytime surveyor of news programs and soap operas. Most days he would rise, dress for work, and drive away at his usual time, only to return a few minutes after Bethany left for school, leaving again a few minutes before time for her to return. If dirty dishes were left in the sink, he failed to put them in the dishwasher. If the hampers were filled with dirty clothes, he left them there. His who-cares attitude was driving Mindy crazy. This was not the Chuck she knew.

"Chuck," she would say, trying to hold down her temper, "the least you can do is help out at home!"

But Chuck would only give her a blank stare and nod. Most times she was not even sure he heard her. Each night when she'd come home from her office, those things would still be waiting undone, and she would have to do them. Even Bethany voiced her concern at the way her normally neat-freak father left things these days. But he would laugh and give her a big hug, telling her both he and her mom were too busy with their jobs sometimes to get everything done.

Mindy resented it when he did that. His careless attitude began to rub off on their daughter as Bethany, too, began to leave her bed unmade and clothing lying around.

Each time her mother would mention it to her, she would respond by saying, "Daddy does it. Why don't you get after him?"

Saturday morning was the day Mindy usually did the grocery shopping and had her hair done and a manicure. Several years ago she had cautioned her staff to contact her on weekends only in the case of an emergency. Weekends were family time. But today, with Chuck off visiting his mother in Providence and Bethany spending the day at the church practicing for an upcoming Bible quiz, Mindy found herself breaking her usual routine and going by Michelle's townhouse. As she sat in her car outside the woman's home, she pondered her life. Something had to give. Sooner or later Bethany would catch her father sitting at home during the day instead of going off to work as she thought he had, or sneaking into the guest room to sleep at night, and she'd begin to ask questions to which they had no answers.

Unexpectedly the front door of the townhouse opened, and Michelle came out carrying a big white plastic bag. She circled the sidewalk to where a communal Dumpster stood and tossed the bag inside. Instantly visions of one of those TV detectives scrounging through a suspect's trash came to mind, and Mindy could almost see herself crawling into the trash bin to obtain evidence, her feet dangling over the sides.

Again the door opened, and Michelle reappeared; only this time she made her way to her car, climbed in, and drove off. Mindy checked her watch, waited five minutes, then, swallowing her pride, pushed open her door and ran to the Dumpster. It was nearly three-fourths full. There, on the top of the other trash, sat the white bag. She glanced first one way, then the other, and seeing none of the other residents, she reached in and snatched up the bag and ran to her car, fully expecting to hear the wail of a siren and see a police car come rushing down the street with an officer leaping out, gun drawn, ready to arrest her.

A rush of adrenaline almost made her giddy as she sat in the front seat clutching the bag tightly. It was all she could do to keep from opening it, to see if her bizarre behavior was worth taking the risk, but she restrained herself, preferring to go through it in the privacy of her home. Feeling like a thief who had just stolen the world's largest diamond, she yanked the gearshift into the drive position and hit the gas pedal, squealing her tires in the process.

Once back in her kitchen, she spread an

old worn-out tablecloth onto the floor and dumped out her treasure. Remembering she had a lightweight pair of plastic gloves in the pantry, she pulled them on and plowed into the mass of eggshells, moldy bread, spoiled coffee cream, smelly paper plates, a few pizza boxes, and numerous other nauseating items, her stomach nearly getting the best of her. Undaunted, she swallowed hard and continued, putting items back into the bag one at a time, wishing she had a free hand to hold her nose. Most of the items she found were the things you would expect to find in the average person's trash. "This has turned out to be nothing but an exercise in futility, a pure waste of time," she said aloud. "It was a stupid idea. Whatever possessed me to do something so foolish?"

She stood in the middle of the room, awkwardly holding the bag in her hands. "Now what? How am I going to get rid of this thing? Chuck is always the one who gathers up the trash, deposits it in the trash can, and places it beside the curb. What if he decides, for some unknown reason, to go through it? It certainly wouldn't do for him to find trash belonging to Michelle in our trash can!" She was crossing the kitchen slowly when an idea hit her. "As awkward as it may be, I'll just have to drop off that bag in a Dumpster at the mall!"

As usual, both Chuck and Mindy were at the Sunday morning church service with their daughter, although they were only there because Bethany insisted they attend. Mindy was sure he felt as awkward as she did as they sat next to each other in the silence of the big sanctuary. Try as she may to concentrate on the pastor's message, all she could think about was Chuck with that woman.

Clarisse, who attended their church regularly, caught up with Mindy in the foyer at the close of the service. "I've been meaning to call you. How are you and Chuck doing?"

Mindy let out a sigh. "Not good. He's so discouraged, Clarisse. He has no idea how to go about clearing his name. And I'm no help."

"I'm keeping my ears open, hoping Michelle will slip up and say something that will be of value. She's a smug one. She struts around that office as if she owns the place. No one likes her. Her overconfidence sickens me. I wish she'd quit and leave town."

Mindy gasped. "We don't want that to happen. She's the only one who could tell the truth."

"Then you believe Chuck's side of the story?"

"I'm trying to," Mindy answered, lowering her head to avoid Clarisse's gaze. "But it's so hard. So hard."

Clarisse reached for Mindy's hand and gave it a squeeze. "As I told you, Mindy, Chuck is a good guy. That woman could never convince me he did anything improper with her. Hang in there. He needs you."

Before Mindy could reply, Clarisse disappeared into the milling crowd of worshippers, but her words lingered, making Mindy wonder if perhaps Chuck was telling the truth.

"I have a math test at school today," Bethany told her mother a few days later as she finished her breakfast and pushed her bowl aside.

"You'll do fine. Knowing you, you've probably studied for it." Smiling, Mindy grabbed her jacket from the hook by the kitchen door and dangled her car keys in front of the girl. "I'm ready when you are. I'll go start the car."

"You're going to have to use my car today, Mindy," Chuck said from his place at the breakfast table, handing her his key ring.

"When I went out to get my briefcase out of my car, I noticed your front tire was flat again. I'll change it and have a new one put on for you."

"I should have done it weeks ago. Thanks, Chuck. I'd appreciate it. I have a superbusy day today." She gave him an honest smile as she exchanged keys with him. "I'll be waiting in the car, Bethany."

Chuck sat staring at his daughter a moment later. "Is that red lipstick I see on your mouth?"

Bethany gave him a smile. "I'm nearly thirteen now, Daddy. All my friends wear red lipstick."

"And I don't like that shirt you're wearing either. It's much too short. It shows your belly button. I'm surprised you'd even consider wearing it. I think you'd better go change into something more presentable, and maybe you should take about half of that lipstick off while you're at it."

Bethany gave him a slight glare. "I can't. I'll be late for school."

"No, you won't. You have plenty of time." Chuck rose and with a smile laid his hand on her shoulder. "Look, Princess — I know being a teenager brings on a lot of changes. I just want you to be safe. That's all. Now scoot! Run back into your bedroom like a good girl and do as Daddy asks."

Five minutes later Bethany came back all smiles, without the red lipstick and wearing a turquoise polo shirt. "This better?"

Chuck nodded. "Much better. What took you so long?"

Bethany shrugged. "Nothing."

"Run along. Your mother is waiting."

Since Bethany usually had her backpack and sometimes a sweater and other items that more than filled up the front seat of Chuck's sports car, Mindy tossed her purse into the backseat.

The two giggled and had a pleasant conversation on the way. Mindy never tired of hearing Bethany laugh and tell stories about the things that happened at school. She let her daughter off at the front sidewalk, waved, and hurried on to her office. When she arrived she parked the car and reached into the backseat for her purse. But when she yanked on the shoulder strap, everything she kept stored inside tumbled out onto the seat, helter-skelter. *Oh, I forgot to zip the zipper!*

With a glance at her watch, she leaped out the door, turned, and began shoving her belongings back into her purse. Finding her compact and her lipstick missing, she ran her hand down the back of the seat cushion to retrieve them. She found them easily, but she also found something else.

A silver and turquoise bracelet, one she'd never seen before.

Instantly red flags began to wave in her mind. *Michelle! The bracelet must belong to Michelle!*

Chapter Five

Her hands shaking, Mindy stared at the bracelet. Had Chuck been lying to her all this time? Was he guilty of the charge Michelle had made against him? Just the thought of her husband and that woman in the backseat of his car made her want to vomit.

Filled with disgust, her eyes dripping with tears of both hurt and disappointment, Mindy clutched the bracelet in her hand and headed for home. All thoughts of her early appointments and her staff waiting for her at the medical office for the customary Monday morning staff meeting vanished as she drove over the speed limit toward their house.

Chuck was still sitting at the kitchen table in his pajamas when she burst through the door. "What are you —"

"Whose bracelet is this?" she shouted at him angrily, waving it in his face. "It sure isn't mine!"

He gave her a mystified look. "I have no idea! I've never seen it before. Where did you get it, and why are you so angry?"

Chafing at his look of innocence, Mindy spat out, "Wedged down in the backseat of your car, that's where!"

Chuck took the bracelet from her hand and examined it. "Maybe it's Bethany's."

She jerked it from him and snarled, "You think I don't know my own daughter's jewelry? I can assure you it does not belong to Bethany!"

Obviously angered by her harsh demeanor and her accusations, Chuck stood quickly and glared at her, his hands planted on his hips. "Are you insinuating Michelle was in the backseat of my car? With me?"

Mindy glared back, her own anger at the boiling point. "Was she?"

Chuck's eyes narrowed, and his face grew red as the little muscle in his jaw ticked with irritation. "I won't dignify that question with an answer."

She seethed at his evasive response. "I've asked you a simple question, Chuck. All it needs is a simple yes or no."

"No!"

"And you expect me to believe that?"

"What you choose to believe is up to you."

Chuck headed toward the family room, stopping in the archway to turn and say in a soft voice, "I only hope you know me well enough to make the right choice. If my own wife doesn't believe me, why should anyone else?"

Mindy dropped into a chair at the table, feeling both physically and mentally drained. She wanted so much to believe Chuck, but how could she? So far everything seemed to point to his guilt. Everything, except what Clarisse had said about Michelle the day Mindy visited her at his office. Surely, if Chuck were innocent, there would be some way to prove it.

The next few weeks were miserable for both Mindy and Chuck. They fought anytime they spoke to each other, except when Bethany was in their presence. At those times they carried on as normally as possible, not wanting to upset her with harsh words.

To Mindy's dismay, Chuck spent most of his days hanging around the house in either his pajamas and robe or the grubbiest old clothes he owned, sitting in front of the TV listening to the same news stories over and over, watching sports and soap operas. Sometimes he would piddle around in the garage trying to repair an old toaster or some such gadget — shaving and dressing just before Bethany came home from school.

"Why don't you go and talk to Jake, plead your case again, and ask him to take you off suspension? At least let him know you're interested in coming back to work," Mindy told him one Saturday morning as she straightened the house and gathered up the laundry. "You're certainly not worth much around here. You could help with the household chores instead of" — she paused and rolled her eyes — "instead of whatever you do, or don't do, around here all day."

Chuck hiked his shoulders. "What good would it do, Mindy? Like you, Jake has his mind made up. He prefers to believe that woman rather than me, the guy who has faithfully worked for him all these years."

"You've turned into a couch potato, Chuck. Look at you. I barely recognize you. You've quit exercising. You're edgy and short on patience. You never go out of the house. This place is in total disarray, with old newspapers, magazines, and such scattered everywhere. Something has to change, or we'll all go crazy! I can't keep covering up for you in front of Bethany."

He shook his head and fumbled with the stubble on his chin. "You don't know what this is doing to me, Mindy. My life is out of

91

control, and I can't find a way to get it back on track."

"Get yourself cleaned up! Go out and find a job, even if it's being a greeter at a department store. Something — anything — that might restore your self-esteem and get you out of the house."

"I've tried, sweetheart — honestly I have. But every employer I've spoken with has asked me for references. Jake is sure to tell them I'm on suspension and the reason why. Would you hire me if you heard I'd been suspended because a coworker accused me of molesting her?"

Mindy did not have to answer. She knew her face told it all.

"I've never been this discouraged in my entire life," Chuck admitted, leaning back in the chair and locking his hands behind his head. "I want my old life back. You and I had a good thing going. Now it's all gone. Sometimes I think everyone, especially you and Bethany, would be better off if I'd just disappear."

Mindy's blood ran cold. The idea of Chuck disappearing from their lives, with no idea of where to find him, frightened her. She had never considered he might do anything that drastic.

Chuck stood slowly to his feet and headed

off toward the guest room. "I'm no good to anyone, least of all you."

The words repeated in her head. *I'm no good to anyone, least of all you.*

The ringing of the doorbell cut into her thoughts. She considered not answering it. She certainly was not in the mood for neighborly chit-chat if it was that nice Mrs. Greeley from next door. But since both cars were in the driveway, it was obvious someone was at home. Trying to force her emotions to settle down, she moved slowly to the door.

"Hello, Mindy. I'm Janine Porter." A pretty, dark-haired woman stood on the other side of the storm door smiling at her, holding a plate of cookies. "My husband, Jim, and I live across the street. We moved in about three months ago. We've met Bethany, but we've never met her mother and father. She's such a delightful child. We're both crazy about her, especially Jim. I thought it was about time we met her parents." She lifted the plate toward Mindy. "I made these for you."

Though Mindy wished the woman had come at a better time, she summoned a smile and pushed open the door, accepting the cookies. "Where are my manners? Please come in."

93

The woman held up a hand. "No, I need to get back — maybe another time. Perhaps we can all go to dinner some evening."

"It was very thoughtful of you to bring these. You said you've met our daughter?"

The woman nodded. "Oh, yes, Bethany found our dog and returned him to us when we first moved in. Those two took a real shine to each other. She's stopped to visit with him several times. She's even helped Jim teach Cocky a few tricks."

"Oh, you're the ones with the cute cocker spaniel. Bethany has mentioned you a number of times. It's nice to meet you. I hope she hasn't been a bother. That girl loves animals. Especially cute little dogs."

Janine shook her head. "A bother? Not at all. We love having her around. In fact, if we had our way, we'd see her more often. You have a lovely, well-mannered daughter. You and Mr. O'Connor should be very proud of her."

Mindy's heart swelled with pride. "We are. Bethany is the delight of our life."

"We don't have children yet. We've only been married a few months, but someday we will. We both love children, but Jim keeps reminding me not all children are as pretty or as well behaved as your daughter."

"Thank you for the compliments. I'll pass

them on to Chuck. That's my husband."

Continuing to smile, the woman backed off the porch. "Well, it's been nice meeting you, Mindy. I hope we can become friends."

"Me, too. Thanks again for the cookies. I'm sure we'll enjoy them."

Janine gave her a wave as she turned to cross the street. "You're welcome. See you later."

Mindy watched her go, deciding it would be nice to get acquainted with their new neighbors. She wondered about Janine's husband. She hoped Jim Porter would be as nice as his wife.

"Mom, can I go home with Tracie after school so we can work on our homework together? I know you have a dinner meeting with someone," Bethany asked when she called her mother during lunch break the next day. "Her mom said it's okay. Her dad is going to drive us to play rehearsal."

Mindy smiled into the phone. "That someone I'm meeting is the chairman of the board. We have to finalize the information for the yearly stockholders' meeting."

"Whatever."

Mindy could almost see her child's face as she used her favorite overworked word. "It's fine with me, honey. Just make sure

95

you get that homework done. What time is play rehearsal over? I'll pick you up."

"Probably by nine."

"I'll be waiting at the main door. See you at nine."

"Line two!" Erica, one of the secretaries, called out as soon as Mindy hung up the phone. "The chairman of the board. He said he needs to change the time for your dinner meeting."

Ever the competent employee, Mindy quickly answered line two. "Changing the time will be no problem," she told the man. She was sure Chuck could pick up Bethany in her place. "I'll meet you at seven thirty at the restaurant."

She tried the house and, guessing he had gone to the grocery store or maybe to get a haircut, left her message on the answering machine, asking him to pick up Bethany at nine.

She planned to call again and remind him after she reached the restaurant, but the chairman and his wife were already waiting for her when she arrived. The three had a lovely dinner as they talked over some business dealings and discussed the agenda for the yearly meeting. He even hinted he thought it was about time they gave Mindy a nice big increase in salary. It was ten after nine and pouring down rain by the time Mindy left the restaurant and crawled into her car. She was tempted to drive by the school, but knowing Chuck and his tendency to be early wherever he went, she headed on home. Sure enough, his car was in the driveway. He and Bethany were already there.

After gathering up the few papers she'd brought home to go over and slipping them into her briefcase, she opened her umbrella and ran the few steps to the porch. Mindy let out a loud gasp as she entered the house. Chuck was in his pajamas, sitting in his recliner, staring at the TV! "Where's Bethany? You did pick her up, didn't you?" she screamed at him as she tossed her briefcase onto a chair and rushed to his side, yanking the remote from his hands.

He gave her a dazed look. "You said you were going to pick her up."

"Chuck!" She grabbed on to his sleeve, giving it a hard shake. "No! I asked you to do it. I left a message on the answering machine. Didn't you get it?"

"I've been home all day! Why would I check the answering machine?" He sat up straight, his eyes wild, the footrest on his chair plummeting down with a loud thud.

"You weren't here when I called!" She felt

herself trembling.

"I was here! I never left the house, not once! I did go out into the garage to find a screwdriver, but I was only gone a few minutes!"

Mindy raced toward the door. "It's nine thirty, Chuck! Our child has been waiting nearly thirty minutes, and you know how she hates storms! I'm going after her."

"I'll go with you."

"No, you stay here. She might try to call!"

Paying no attention to the speed limit, Mindy raced her car toward the school, pulling up to the front entrance in record time despite the heavy downpour. But with the exception of the security lights, the school was dark, and not a soul was in sight. Not taking time to grab her umbrella, she pushed open the door and ran up the steps, banging loudly on the glass with her fists and calling out Bethany's name.

But Bethany didn't answer.

Lightning flashed across the sky, and thunder rolled overhead, giving the night an eerie look.

Not sure what else to do or where to turn, Mindy pounded on the door again and again, continuing to scream out Bethany's name. Finally, a face appeared behind the glass — a weathered face — framed by scraggly white hair. "I can't find my daughter!" Mindy yelled out as the man unlocked the door and pushed it open a crack. "I was supposed to pick her up at nine."

"No one here now," the man, who explained he was the night watchman, said sympathetically. "A girl was waiting when I made my rounds about a half hour ago. I offered to let her wait inside, but she refused to come in. Said her mom would be here any second. She was gone when I checked about twenty minutes later."

Mindy watched helplessly as he closed the door and disappeared into the darkness. Grabbing her cell phone from the holster on her waistband, she frantically dialed Tracie's number.

"She was still waiting for you when my mom picked me up, Mrs. O'Connor," the girl told her. "We offered to take her home, but she wouldn't go. She said she was supposed to wait for you."

Mindy punched the end button and dialed her home number. Chuck answered on the first ring.

"She's not at the school! Have you heard from her?" she yelled into the phone, trying to make herself heard above the claps of thunder belching overhead.

"No, I was hoping she was still there."

Mindy began to cry. Where was Bethany? Her baby? Her only child? "Oh, Chuck, if only you'd checked the answering machine!"

Chuck clutched the phone tightly between his palms, his mind in a whir. "I'm calling the police," he told her in a take-charge manner. "Stay right where you are. I'm coming over there."

After phoning, without even taking time to change from his pajamas into jeans and a T-shirt, Chuck grabbed his jacket and his keys from the hall table and ran to his car. He arrived at the school in a matter of minutes, as two police officers moved up onto the porch. Mindy was crying hysterically and trying to explain what had happened. He joined in the conversation but found he was of no more help than his wife.

Mindy flailed an accusing finger in his face. "He was supposed to pick our daughter up after play rehearsal, but he —"

"I would have if I'd known my wife put a message on the answering machine," Chuck countered, feeling guilty for letting Mindy and his daughter down.

The officer who was doing most of the questioning held up his hand between them. "Look, folks — I know you're both upset, but let's quit all this blaming and concentrate on finding your daughter." Turning to Mindy, he asked, "Have you contacted her friends or anyone she might have ridden home with?"

Mindy nodded. "There's only one person she would have ridden with, her best friend, and I've already called her. She said Bethany was still here when she left."

"And you've talked to the night watchman, right?"

Again she nodded. "Yes, he said she was here when he checked about ten after nine. He tried to get her to wait inside out of the rain, but she refused. When he —"

"When he checked about twenty minutes later," Chuck inserted, pulling his wife into his arms and pressing her head against his chest, "she was gone. We've cautioned Bethany over and over not to accept rides from people she doesn't know. I can't imagine she'd accept a ride with a stranger."

"The best thing you folks can do for your daughter is go on home. She may be trying to call you right now," the officer said kindly.

"She has my cell phone number." Mindy's flattened palm went to her waist. "She knows I keep it with me at all times. Why hasn't she called me?"

"I don't know, ma'am, but there is nothing you can do here. You need to start calling all her friends, her teachers, your neighbors, anyone who may know of her whereabouts."

Chuck wiped the rain from his face with the back of his hand. "What about the night watchman? It seems he was the last one to see her. Shouldn't you talk to him?"

"That's exactly what we plan to do, sir." The officer nodded his head in Mindy's direction. "I suggest Mrs. O'Connor go on home and wait by the phone, in case your daughter tries to call there. I'll have another officer follow her and stay with her. You can stay and cruise the neighborhood with me." He placed a consoling hand on Mindy's shoulder. "We'll do our best to help you find your daughter, ma'am. Both my partner and I are parents. We know what you're going through."

Less than ten minutes later, Mindy and the officer entered the house on Victor Lane. She let out a shriek of joy when the phone was ringing and hurried to answer it.

"Mrs. O'Connor, this is Tracie's mother. I was concerned about Bethany and wanted to see if you'd found her yet."

Aching with disappointment, Mindy braced herself against the desk, her hand on her forehead. "We were hoping this was a call from her."

"I'm so sorry. I'll get off the line. Please let us know if we can do anything to help."

After thanking the woman for her concern, she placed the phone back in its cradle.

"Mrs. O'Connor, try to concentrate," the officer said. "Is there anyone else your daughter might have trusted enough to ride home with? A neighbor, maybe a friend you haven't seen in a long time? Possibly an older boy she met at school?"

"No, of course not! She's not quite thirteen. She's certainly not old enough to be thinking about boys!"

He gave her a slight grin. "My daughter is thirteen, and she's plenty interested in boys."

Mindy pulled off her jacket and sank down on the sofa. "Maybe I don't know my daughter as well as I thought, but I doubt she'd do something like this, knowing we were coming to pick her up."

"Even if everyone else had gone and she was the only one standing there in the rain?" he prodded gently.

"Maybe, if it was someone she thought she could trust. She's terribly frightened by storms," she conceded, hating to consider such a thing but knowing there was a slight possibility something like that had occurred. "Sometimes when the weather is bad, she's so frightened she crawls into bed with us."

She listened as the officer used his cell phone to call in and report his whereabouts, then waited, hoping he would have something to tell her.

"My partner and your husband are still combing the neighborhood," he explained as he fastened the phone back in the holster on his heavy black belt.

Mindy stared at the clock on the desk. It was well past ten. Flashes of lightning still brightened the room, and thunder continued to roll overhead. Wherever Bethany was, she had to be terrified.

At eleven Chuck and another man he introduced as Captain Wyatt appeared at the door. Mindy threw herself into her husband's arms and pressed her face against his chest. "Oh, Chuck, you didn't find her?"

He shook his head sadly. "No, but we'll keep looking."

"It's your fault!" Now in hysterics, Mindy beat her fists against his chest. "You were supposed to pick her up! Can't I count on you for anything?"

Filled with more guilt than Mindy could ever heap on him, Chuck grabbed on to her wrists and held them tightly in his grasp. "Look — there's nothing you can say to me I haven't already said to myself. You're right. I should have checked the answering machine, and I should have picked her up! If anything has happened to our precious Bethany, I'll — I'll —" Slowly he released his hold; then, tilting his wife's chin up and meeting her gaze with his, he whispered softly, "We'll find her, Mindy. We have to."

The two jumped when the doorbell rang and two additional officers entered their home. One of them, a woman, introduced herself as Lieutenant Terry and gestured toward the sofa. "Please sit down. I need to ask you some questions."

Mindy's eyes widened. "Why? We've already told you what we know. Shouldn't you be out looking for our daughter?"

Chuck cradled the small of her back with his hand. "Let's do what she says. Maybe we'll think of something that might help."

Once the three were seated, the lieutenant pulled a pad from the case she was carrying and made a few notes. Then, looking at them in a kind, understanding way, she asked, "Has your daughter been upset about anything lately? Maybe been grounded for having low grades or for not coming home on time?"

Mindy's eyes flashed. "No! Not Bethany! She's a model student. Makes straight A's!"

The woman scribbled a few notes, then turned to them again. "Has she ever run away from home or threatened to run away?"

"No!" Chuck answered firmly. "Not once. Bethany is a happy, easygoing child who rarely complains about anything."

Lieutenant Terry peered at them over her half-glasses. "That may be so, but your child is missing, and it's nearly midnight. You have to give us something to go on. We need your complete honesty here. Is there anything going on in your family that might affect your daughter? A fight between the two of you? Money problems? Maybe a job situation?"

Mindy cast a quick glance at Chuck.

"I've been suspended from my job, but Bethany doesn't know. We haven't told her yet."

"Maybe you only think she doesn't know. Kids are often more perceptive than we realize."

Captain Wyatt moved up beside Lieutenant Terry, his thumbs locked into his belt. "You said suspended. What exactly does that mean?"

Chuck's gut hurt as he drew in a deep

breath. "I was falsely accused of something."

"Must have been pretty serious for your boss to place you on suspension." The man stood waiting for Chuck's explanation.

"One of the women in our office accused me of —" He swallowed hard, finding it impossible to say the word.

"Of what, Mr. O'Connor?"

The look on Mindy's face broke Chuck's heart.

"Of molesting her."

"And you're sure your daughter doesn't know about this?"

"We've been keeping it from her," Mindy said. "We're trying to find a way to prove my husband's innocence."

Her words of support surprised Chuck, and he suddenly didn't feel as alone anymore. "I didn't do it. Honest, I didn't," he said adamantly. "I have no idea why she would accuse me of such a thing."

The officers cast a glance at one another, which Chuck interpreted as saying they doubted his story.

"I'll need several recent photos of your daughter," Lieutenant Terry said, rising. "And we'll need to know if she has any distinguishing marks, like a birthmark or an unusually placed mole, and a description of what she was wearing."

Once the officers had each been given a recent snapshot of Bethany, along with a description of her clothing, they conferred with one another, then left to continue their search, leaving Lieutenant Terry behind. "I'll be staying with you," she told them. "Just in case you get a phone call."

"From Bethany?" Mindy asked quickly, feeling a new ray of hope.

The officer frowned slightly. "Her or anyone else who may know her whereabouts."

"You think someone has taken her?" Mindy nearly screamed out. "Kidnapped our daughter? But why?"

"No, I'm not saying that, Mrs. O'Connor, but we have to be realistic. Your daughter has been missing for several hours now. From what you tell me, she is not the type of child who would stay out with friends without telling you or run away from home. The best thing you and Mr. O'Connor can do is try to come up with the names of others who may know of Bethany's whereabouts."

"But we don't —"

"Why don't you fix a pot of coffee, Mrs. O'Connor? I think we could all use a cup."

"I'll help you," Chuck said, sensing his wife's need and wanting to comfort her.

"Coffee sounds good."

The lights blinked as a gigantic clap of thunder roared overhead. Mindy grabbed on to Chuck's arm and melded herself to him, her tears flowing freely. "Oh, Chuck, where is Bethany? Where is our baby girl? Is she huddling somewhere, terrified of the storm?"

She paused, her eyes rounded with fear, then let out a pitiful cry that ripped at Chuck's heart. "Or is she going through something much worse?"

CHAPTER SIX

The morning dawned gray and cloudy, with an almost ominous feeling. Sleep had eluded Mindy, as well as Chuck, each crash of thunder and each bolt of lightning bringing on a new set of fears. Over ten hours had passed since their daughter disappeared. Ten long, painful hours, and the wear and tear of the experience was showing as they huddled together in the semidarkness of the family room, waiting, hoping for the phone to ring or the door to open and Bethany to come walking through.

But it did not happen.

Mindy's mother arrived from Newport about seven, her face tired and haggard from her all-night vigil near her phone.

By eight they had received more than six calls from radio and TV stations or newspapers that had heard about Bethany's disappearance and wanted to do stories on it.

By nine Mindy left her mother in charge of the phone and joined the search with Chuck, going from house to house in the four-block area around their home, personally begging their neighbors for any scrap of information that might lead them to Bethany.

Though several people told the two how much they loved their daughter and what a sweet kid she was, none of them offered any concrete information. Not even Treva Jordan, Bethany's Sunday school teacher and mentor, or Tracie, her best friend, who had attended the play rehearsal with her, could think of anything to help. Though several of her classmates remembered seeing Bethany on the porch, waiting for her parents after the practice, none of them had actually seen her leave.

"Jim and I will be glad to help in any way we can," Janine Porter told them when Mindy appeared at her door asking about Bethany. "You name it — we'll do it."

"Thanks," Mindy told her as she backed off the porch, pulling her jacket collar up around her neck. "If some news doesn't turn up soon, we may have to ask you to help us canvass a larger area. Someone in Warren has to have seen our daughter."

"Are you planning to pass out flyers or

put up posters around the community? I could help with that, and I'm sure Jim will want to help, too. He's home today. He wanted to play golf all day, but I refused to let him go. It might sound silly, but I'm afraid to stay home alone. I had to shed a few tears to accomplish it, but I actually managed to keep him here. I told him if he went, I was going with him. That kept him here. He knows what a terrible golfer I am." Janine rambled on, seemingly uncomfortable and unsure what to say.

"At this point I'm not sure what we should do next. Almost everyone we've talked to has offered to help in any way they can. We just keep hoping Bethany will call and say she's all right."

"Oh, Mindy, I'm praying that will happen."

"So am I, Janine. So am I."

Chuck was waiting for her at the corner. "No one knows anything," he said sadly, his tone somber.

Mindy slipped her hand into the crook of his arm and let out a sigh. "I didn't get anywhere either. Now what?"

"I think it's time to talk to Captain Wyatt again." Chuck pulled out his cell phone, dialed, and waited for an answer.

Mindy wept softly as she listened to the one-sided conversation, all the while her mind fixed on Bethany.

"Let's go," Chuck said after placing his phone back in his pocket. "He's going to meet us at the house."

Mindy's mother met them at the door with reddened eyes and an anxious look on her face. "Any news?"

Both Mindy and Chuck shook their heads.

"Captain Wyatt is in the kitchen," Mrs. Carson said, brushing away a tear from her cheek. "He's such a nice man. I know he's doing everything he can to help find our little girl."

"She's not a little girl anymore, Mom," Mindy said, wiping her eyes with a tissue as she followed her into the kitchen. "She's a lovely, responsible teenager. I'm so afraid some —"

"Now, dear, don't be thinking those kinds of thoughts." Her mother took her by the arm and motioned her toward a chair at the kitchen table. "I'm going to fix you a piece of toast. I'll bet you haven't eaten a thing today. You must keep your strength up."

Chuck extended his hand as he entered the kitchen. "Any word?"

Captain Wyatt rose with a shake of his

head. "Sorry. No. If we don't hear something soon, you two might want to consider doing an interview and showing pictures of Bethany on one of the Providence TV station's news reports. I'm sure they'd send one of their reporters and cameramen here to do it."

"It has to be the night watchman," Chuck replied, trying desperately to come up with a viable solution to his daughter's disappearance. "She knew him. She might have gone inside with him."

"The man has been at that school for nearly thirty years. His reputation is impeccable. There's never been a single complaint lodged against him. He's sick about this and has offered to help in any way he can."

"But he might be covering up," Chuck insisted.

The captain nodded. "Yes, he might be, but so far nothing has indicated he is."

"Who else could have had the opportunity?"

He motioned for Chuck to come closer, then said in a low voice, "I don't want your wife to hear this, but I have to tell you. Thirteen is the prime predator target age. You can't imagine how many thirteen-year-olds have twenty-two-year-old boyfriends, and their moms and dads are clueless."

Chuck winced, his mouth suddenly going dry. "Bethany has never even had a boy-friend!"

"As I said, parents often have no idea what is going on with their daughters when they are supposed to be spending the night with a friend or attending one of those slumber-party things. I just thought you should know."

"I'd never even considered something like that. Though Bethany is maturing, she's still very young. I guess I hadn't realized my baby is no longer a baby."

"Mr. O'Connor, in cases where a child is actually abducted —"

Chuck felt his heart clench at the word. "Abducted? You really think someone has taken our daughter?"

With another glance toward Mindy, who was still in conversation with her mother, Captain Wyatt went on. "Your daughter has been missing since last night. It's a possibil-ity we have to consider at this point. Any-thing you can remember, even the tiniest thing, maybe a comment Bethany made or some type of unusual behavior, might be valuable to us as we search for her."

Shocked by the idea of someone taking Bethany, Chuck felt himself reel. He wanted to ask the captain much more but dropped the subject when his wife approached with a fresh cup of coffee.

"Wh–what are you two talking about?"

"Just going over a few things." Captain Wyatt stretched first one arm and then the other, gazing at Mindy for a moment before going on. "I hate to ask this again, ma'am, but are you absolutely sure your daughter hasn't run away? Statistically, that's what happens with most missing teenagers."

"No, not our Bethany!" Mindy rubbed the back of her hand across her sunken eyes, smearing bits of mascara onto her cheeks. "You don't know her. She'd never run away."

The captain gave his head a sad shake. "I hope you're right. It's tough to find a girl who doesn't want to be found. Too many people out there who are willing to help her hide."

The ringing of the doorbell sent Mindy racing to the door, with Chuck following close behind.

"Hi," Janine said with a smile. "When I told my husband I'd offered to help you, he suggested we come right over."

"Hi, I'm Jim Porter." The man opened the storm door and stuck his hand through. "I've heard so much about the two of you from Bethany. It's nice to finally meet you."

Chuck gave the man's hand a vigorous shake.

"That girl said you two are the best parents ever." The smile left the man's face as they moved inside and Chuck closed the door. "You guys have to be worn out. Janine said you've been helping the police canvass the neighborhood."

Weeping quietly, Mindy motioned them to the sofa and chairs in front of the crackling blaze in the fireplace. "We are, but we have to keep going, for Bethany's sake. We stopped long enough for a cup of coffee. Can I get you some?"

"No thanks." Jim nodded toward Captain Wyatt, who had come into the room. "Is there any news at all?"

The man gave him a slight frown. "We're still hoping to hear from her."

"So," Jim said, briskly rubbing his hands together, "tell us what we can do."

"Jim suggested putting posters up all over town with Bethany's picture on them," Janine said. "I think that sounds like a good idea, don't you, Chuck?"

Chuck nodded. "Sure wouldn't hurt."

"I can make the posters for you," Jim volunteered. "I'm pretty good on the computer. All you have to do is let me know what you want the text to say. If you can give me a recent picture of Bethany, I'll scan it in, then take the whole thing to the copy center and have it blown up in color."

"That's very kind of you," Mindy replied, blotting at her eyes. "We can't thank you enough for wanting to help."

Jim stood and hurried across the room to the desk, pulling out the chair. "Chuck, you come over here and write what you want the poster to say while Mindy gets me Bethany's picture, and I'll get right on it."

Fifteen minutes later, after Captain Wyatt approved the wording for the posters, the Porters were out the door with the promise the posters would be ready by four o'clock and they would help put them up all over town.

"They seem like a nice couple," Mindy said, blowing her nose as she gazed out the window, watching the pair cross the street. "It's amazing how willing people are to help one another in a crisis."

"It sure is." Chuck moved up close and slipped an arm about her waist. "Why don't you stay here and rest? I'll start knocking on doors over on Water Street."

Mindy took one final glance out the window before turning to face her husband, her sobs uncontrollable. "I'll go with you. I don't care how tired we are; we have to spend every minute looking for our daughter. No telling where she is, Chuck, but I know wherever she is, she's frightened, and I can't rest until we find her."

After an uneventful afternoon of knocking on doors, Chuck walked with Mindy into their house just minutes before the Porters arrived with the stack of posters.

"I added a brightly colored border," Jim said, pulling several posters from the stack and placing them on the coffee table. "I thought they might attract more attention that way. And I also had some flyers made that we could pass out to everyone we meet."

Mindy picked up one and touched her finger to her daughter's picture. "My beautiful Bethany," she said in a teary whisper. "I love you so much."

Chuck took her hand and linked his fingers with hers. "We'll find her, babe. Have faith."

She whirled into him and pressed her face to his chest. "Faith? I don't know how to have faith. I wish I'd paid attention to Pastor Park's words all those Sundays we attended church with our daughter. She's the one who has faith. I wish I knew how to pray like Bethany does."

"Wherever she is, she's fine, sweetheart.

We have to believe that."

"I do believe it, Chuck. Honest I do, but it's been so long. Where could she be? Is she cold? Hungry? Frightened? Is she calling out to us for help?"

"You can't talk like that," Janine said, putting an arm around her shoulders. "It's not good for you or for her."

"I say we get these posters up as soon as we can." Jim divided the stack in half. "A couple of our neighbors have volunteered to help, too. We'll take part of the stack to them so they can get started. I think we should put them in any store windows we can, tack them to posts, place them wherever there's a spot, besides giving the small flyers to everyone we see." He pulled a folded piece of paper from his pocket, laying it on the table before them. "I've made a rough map of the area. Chuck, if you and Mindy take this small part from here to the east edge of town, Janine and I and the other volunteers will take care of the rest. If we haven't heard something by tomorrow, I'll have more posters printed, and we'll fan out even farther."

"You don't mind staying by the phone?" Mindy asked her mother.

"Not at all, dear. You two get those posters up. That's the important thing right now.

If I hear anything at all, I'll call you on your cell phone."

Three hours later, feeling discouraged, Mindy stood in front of the bathroom mirror holding a warm washcloth to her face, trying to soothe her jangled nerves. Every bone in her body ached. But the worst ache of all was in her heart. Her baby girl was still missing, and they had not found one shred of evidence as to where she was or whom she was with.

Though she had tried, other than the piece of dry toast she'd eaten for breakfast, she hadn't had a thing all day except for countless cups of hot coffee.

After drying her hands and rubbing on a bit of lotion, Mindy walked slowly down the hall. Never had she felt so helpless. There seemed to be nothing else to do other than what she had already done. Her efforts seemed futile.

"Feeling any better?" Chuck asked as she sat down beside him on the sofa. "You really ought to get some sleep."

"Sleep?" Mindy snapped at him, the strain of the situation telling on her. "With my daughter missing, you think I can sleep?"

"Dear, Chuck is as upset about this as you are," Mrs. Carson told her daughter, reaching to pat her hand.

Turning to her husband, Mindy rallied a slight smile. "I'm sorry, Chuck. I had no business jumping at you like that. I know you love her as much as I do."

Without a word he slipped an arm around her and pulled her close, planting a kiss on her forehead.

Lieutenant Terry studied her clipboard for a moment, then checked her watch before raising her narrowed eyes to the pair. "It's after nine o'clock. Your daughter has been missing for twenty-four hours. I know you've checked her room, but it's time we do a thorough search."

Mindy leaned forward with a frown. "Why? I've already told you what she was wearing."

Captain Wyatt stood, locking his thumbs into his belt. "Lieutenant Terry is right. A thorough search of that room needs to be done now."

"Bethany's room is hers. In this house we respect one another's privacy."

Lieutenant Terry's brows climbed a notch. "You mean, Mrs. O'Connor, you never go into her room?"

"Of course I do," Mindy said defensively. "I take the clothes out of her hamper, and after they're washed I hang them in her closet and place the other things on her bed so she can put them where she wants them."

"You never take a peek in her drawers? Or check out what CDs she plays?"

"I've never felt the need to do those things. Bethany is a model child."

The officers gave each other guarded glances.

Chuck stood, his shoulders slumping. "You'd have to know our daughter to understand what my wife is saying. I can't even remember the last time we had to discipline Bethany."

"That may well be, and I'm sure you're telling the truth about Bethany, but she is almost thirteen, and from my experience," Lieutenant Terry said in a sympathetic voice, "girls that age are eager to try their wings. Plus, they're easily influenced by their peers. It's estimated over a million young people run away from home every year."

Mindy stared at her, unable to comprehend such a vast number. "Surely that's not true."

Lieutenant Terry nodded. "Yes, ma'am, I'm afraid it's not only true, but many runaways go unreported because the parents are too embarrassed to admit it or they're glad to have the children out of their hair."

Captain Wyatt stepped forward, nodding his head in the direction of the hall. "Why don't we have a look at her room? More than likely we won't find a thing. But if something there would give us the slightest clue, I'm sure you'd want us to find it, right?"

Both Mindy and Chuck gave a nod of surrender. Chuck led the way, with Mindy following and the two officers behind her.

"She loves pink," Mindy said as she sat down on Bethany's bed, sobbing. "We did this room just the way she wanted it."

"Did she spend much time in her room, Mrs. O'Connor?" Lieutenant Terry asked as her eyes surveyed the room's contents.

"Oh, yes," Mindy said proudly. "She loved this room. Most evenings she did her homework in here."

Captain Wyatt picked up a Bible from the nightstand. "This hers?"

Chuck nodded. "Yes, Bethany is a Christian, and she's on the church's quiz team. You wouldn't believe how many verses of Scripture she's memorized."

"How about this jewelry box?" Lieutenant Terry asked, picking it up and handing it toward Mindy. "I know you said you've already checked it once, but would you take another look? Is anything missing? A piece of jewelry she was particularly fond of or one that had a special meaning to her?"

Mindy lifted the lid and fingered through the contents. "No, not that I'm aware of." She pulled a fine gold chain from the box and held it up for them to see. "This was what she loved most. This gold chain with the tiny diamond cross on it. Her father gave it to her on her twelfth birthday. That just shows you she didn't run away. She'd never leave it behind."

"Has she had this computer long?" Lieutenant Terry pressed the ON button and watched as the computer booted up and the screen illuminated. "I noticed you had a computer on the desk in the family room. Is this her personal computer? Does anyone else use it?"

"No, she's the only one." Mindy watched as the woman pulled out Bethany's desk chair and sat down. "Is something wrong?"

"I just want to have a look and see what sorts of things she keeps on here."

"I'm not sure Bethany would want you doing that."

"Even if it will help us find her if she's in trouble?" Lieutenant Terry asked, her eyes fixed on the screen.

Captain Wyatt pulled out the top drawer of a tall chest. "Does she keep a diary?"

"She used to, but I don't think she does anymore. I never see her writing in one." It irritated Mindy to see them going through her daughter's things in this way, but she kept her silence.

"Where did she keep it when she was writing in it?" the captain asked. "In one of these drawers?"

"I'm not sure," Mindy conceded.

The officer motioned toward the chest. "I think you'd prefer to handle her personal items yourself, ma'am. Would you come over here and lift the things out of the drawers one at a time?"

Mindy sent Chuck a bewildered look, and when he nodded she moved up next to the officer and began removing Bethany's things from the drawer. When they finally reached the bottom, he told her she could put them back in. They continued the procedure until each of the drawers in the chest, the nightstands, the dresser, and a small cabinet had been searched.

Captain Wyatt closed the last drawer and stood back, looking disappointed. "Well, it doesn't look like there's anything here to help us."

"I may have something." Lieutenant Terry stared at the screen as she made a slight move of the mouse. "Have you ever heard your daughter mention someone she calls Trustworthy?"

Both Mindy and Chuck shook their heads as they moved up to stand behind her.

"I'm not sure yet, but I found a folder marked TRUSTWORTHY. That's a pretty unusual name. Like a name one would use as a nickname or a screen name in a chat room or on one of those instant-message programs."

Captain Wyatt placed his hand on the desk and leaned over her, peering at the screen. "Are there any documents in the folder?"

"Only one."

"What does it say?"

"It's a short message. Looks like it has been copied and pasted from somewhere else. It's time stamped. I have my computer set up the same way."

"Time stamped?" Chuck asked, looking confused. "What does that mean?"

"When you talk on one of those instant-message services, you can set your computer to list the actual time, right down to the second, along the left side of each entry," Captain Wyatt explained, still bending over the computer.

"I'm not sure you'll want to hear this," Lieutenant Terry said, straightening in the chair.

CHAPTER SEVEN

"The message is from someone named Trustworthy, the name on the folder. He's talking to someone who calls themselves Twinkletoes. I assume that's your daughter, since this is her computer."

Mindy moved closer and gawked at the screen. "I've never heard her mention anyone named Trustworthy."

"How about Twinkletoes?"

Chuck let out a gasp. "That's the nickname I used to call Bethany when she was a little girl, but I rarely call her that now! From the time she could walk, she danced anytime music came on the radio or I played an audio tape!"

"Evidently that's what she chose for her screen name."

Mindy felt light-headed and sick to her stomach. "What does the message say?"

"I won't read it to you line by line, but Trustworthy is telling her he is a talent scout for a major Hollywood movie producer who is looking for a young girl to play the lead part in his upcoming movie. He's telling her he thinks she'd be great for the part, if only she could get to California for an audition."

"She's never mentioned a thing about this to me," Chuck said, backing away from the desk with a questioning glance toward Mindy. "Did she tell you about it?"

Fighting off fresh tears, she shook her head. "Not a word. I can't imagine why. She tells me everything."

"His next line will tell you why," the lieutenant said. "He warns her most parents are reluctant to let their daughters go to Hollywood and become a star. He tells her to keep things quiet, and he'll try to work out a way to pay for her trip. If that works out, then she can tell her parents."

Feeling faint, Mindy grabbed on to the edge of the chest, her head reeling.

After rushing to Mindy's side and wrapping his arm around her waist to support her, Chuck asked, "When was this written?"

Lieutenant Terry paused, as if checking to make sure Mindy was all right before answering. "Two weeks before your daughter disappeared."

The room fell into a petrifying silence, the

steady hum of the computer's hard drive the only sound.

"That's all I've discovered on the computer so far. There may be more. I'll keep looking."

"But you found that one message," Chuck said, looking hopeful. "If she talked to this person, wouldn't all of his messages be on her computer, too?"

Captain Wyatt shook his head. "You must not spend much time on the computer, Mr. O'Connor. Once an instant-message conversation is over, the participants click out of the window, and that conversation is gone forever."

"But that one was on there. How did it stay?"

"She must have wanted to save that one. Your daughter highlighted that portion, hit COPY, transferred it over, and saved it to a document, then put it in this file folder. Unless she has saved others, any talks she had with Trustworthy are not retrievable. But I can have one of the computer geeks we occasionally use take a look at her hard drive. If she's saved others then deleted them, he might be able to find them."

Chuck rubbed at his forehead. "I use computers for a lot of things every day at work, but I guess I know very little about them."

"I — I don't know much about them either. I use the one in the family room only to send e-mail to my friends and family and write a few letters now and then." Mindy sucked in a deep breath of air, hoping it would help her head to clear. "I've never gotten into this message thing. I have no idea how it works. Bethany is our computer whiz."

"Do you suppose this Trustworthy has anything to do with her disappearance?" Chuck asked.

Captain Wyatt shrugged. "Without knowing exactly how chummy the two of them have become, it's hard to say."

His words made Mindy furious. "Bethany would never leave with someone she met on the Internet!"

"Mrs. O'Connor, you have no idea how persuasive these people can be. We're not saying your daughter ran away with him. What we are saying is, we have to explore every possibility. Your daughter has been gone over twenty-four hours now."

"You don't think I'm aware of that?" Mindy barked back. "Don't you people know how hard this is on us?

Mrs. Carson, who had been standing

quietly by the doorway, moved quickly to her daughter and gently took hold of her arm. "You're worn out, dear. You have to get some sleep. Why don't you let me fix you a nice cup of hot tea and —"

Mindy jerked her arm away. "Don't you see, Mother? Until Bethany is found I can't sleep! She may be lying out there somewhere, cold and hungry. How can I sleep without knowing where she is and if she's all right?"

Mrs. Carson backed away with a look of exasperation. "I want Bethany found, too, but you can't keep going without rest. You can't think straight, and your body will rebel."

Mindy felt heartsick at the way she'd snapped at her well-meaning mother. "I'm sorry, Mom. I hope you'll forgive me, but I doubt I'll sleep again until my baby girl is safe at home."

"We haven't searched her closet yet," Lieutenant Terry reminded them. "Maybe something in there will help us. From my experience, girls Bethany's age like to keep mementos in a box or a bag. That'd be a great place to hide anything she didn't want you to see."

Mindy had to bite her tongue to keep from lashing out at the officer. How dare she think Bethany would keep things hidden from her? "I've already told you — all that is missing is the clothing she was wearing last night."

"Let them have a look," Chuck said softly, nudging her toward the mirror closet doors.

She nodded and, following his lead, slid open one of the doors.

"Looks like the typical teenage girl's closet," Lieutenant Terry said. "Filled to the brim. This may take awhile."

Mindy leaned into Chuck's arms as the two stood off to one side and watched as the officers pulled the garments from the rod, one by one, checking the pockets, then placing them on the bed.

Once the rod was emptied, they began taking things from the two overhead shelves, going through numerous shoe boxes and bags, checking the contents of each one before stacking it by the garments.

"Nothing so far," Captain Wyatt said while pulling a rather large box from the back of the top shelf.

"Be careful. Those are her Barbie dolls!" Mindy stepped forward and reached for the box.

Lieutenant Terry moved it from her grasp. "I'll need to check the contents just to make sure there's nothing else here. Sometimes these guys manage to get presents to their intended victims."

"Presents? What kind of presents?"

"Jewelry. Fancy T-shirts. That sort of thing. Those gifts become a tangible bond between the two."

Mindy grabbed hold of Chuck's hand, needing something stable to hold on to. "This is too much! I'm sure Bethany would never take a gift from someone she didn't know."

Captain Wyatt gave a slight shrug. "Let's hope you're right."

Finally, all the clothing had been removed from the rack, and all the shelves had been emptied. Mindy stared at the pile on the bed, her heart breaking. "I was hoping you'd find something."

"We're not through yet." Lieutenant Terry knelt and began taking the many shoes from the closet floor. "Your daughter must like shoes the way my daughter does," she said with a slight snicker.

Mindy gazed at the pile. "Bethany loves shoes. We try to get her a pair for each of her birthdays and Christmas, not to mention the ones her grandmother buys for her or she buys herself."

"Well, that's about it," Lieutenant Terry said, placing the last shoe by its mate. "That pair of cowboy boots is all that's left."

"She loved those boots. We bought them for her at the state fair," Chuck explained as the woman reached into the far back corner of Bethany's closet. "Always kidded me, saying she needed a horse to go with them."

"Oh, oh. What have we here?"

Captain Wyatt quickly squatted down beside his partner. "Got something?"

She nodded as she reached into the boot and pulled out a pink diary. "Looks like our girl kept a diary after all."

Mindy's hand went to her chest as she let out a loud gasp. "I didn't know she was still keeping one!"

Lieutenant Terry rose. "Which probably means there are things in here your daughter would prefer you didn't know."

As Mindy reached for the diary, Captain Wyatt stepped in between the two women. "I'm sorry, Mrs. O'Connor, but your daughter's privacy is no longer a concern here. Why don't you and your husband go on in the other room while we have a look at it?"

Crazed, Mindy pushed past him. "No! If there's anything in that diary that will help us find Bethany, we want to know about it."

"She's right." Chuck took hold of his wife's arm and pulled her out of the way.

"We need to know what's in that diary."

Captain Wyatt shrugged. "Your call." Then, turning to Lieutenant Terry, he said, "Go ahead. Check it out."

The three stood silently, their attention fixed on the woman as she leafed through the pages. Suddenly she stopped on a single page, her brows rising. "Bingo!"

"You found something?" Mindy asked quickly.

The officer nodded. "It appears your daughter and Trustworthy have been carrying on a conversation nearly every night for well over a month. Her first entry about him said she'd met a really nice man on the Internet who was a talent scout. And after he'd asked her a number of questions about her age, her size, and the color of her hair, he told her she sounded like the kind of girl he'd been searching for to play the lead part in a movie."

Mindy clutched at Chuck's arm. "Why didn't she tell us this?"

"I can answer that one." Lieutenant Terry thumbed back a few pages. "She says right here that he told her she shouldn't tell anyone, especially not her parents, because she wouldn't want them to be disappointed if things didn't work out. And he also said that if any of her friends found out about it, they'd all want to be movie stars, too, and he didn't have the time to talk to each one, especially when he felt Bethany would be perfect for the part."

Mindy burst into tears. "How could she have believed him?"

"These guys are pros at this, Mrs. O'Connor. They know what to say to these kids to get them to trust them."

"What else does she say?" Captain Wyatt interjected.

Lieutenant Terry read a few more pages, then lifted her eyes slowly. "He told her he had decided it was time for her to come to Hollywood for an audition. He asked her if she thought her parents would pay for her flight out there and for the hotel room during the week she would have to be there, learning lines and meeting with the movie producers."

"She never said a word to me about this." Chuck gave his head a sad shake.

"Apparently she told him she was sure you would say no because you still thought of her as a baby, instead of a maturing young woman as Trustworthy did."

"She is our baby!" Mindy nearly shouted, her nerves to the breaking point. "She's not even thirteen!"

"Well, she says here that he was so certain

she was right for the part, he decided to pay for things himself. He said —" Lieutenant Terry stopped reading aloud and shot a quick glance toward Captain Wyatt.

"What? What did he say?" Chuck reached his hand toward the diary, but the officer pulled it away.

"He said that since most parents are reluctant to let their daughters become movie stars, it would be best if she didn't tell you he had decided to pay for everything. He told her she should go on to Hollywood with him, and once they were there she could call you and tell you where she was. He'd convinced her that when you heard how much money she was going to make doing the movie, you would be sorry you tried to stand in her way."

"She's with him?" Mindy felt the room swirling about her as the reality of Bethany's words hit her full force. "In California?"

Chuck grabbed on to her and held her fast. "Surely not! Not Bethany. She's so levelheaded! I can't believe she'd go off with a stranger!"

"He may have been a stranger to her, but believe me, he knew all about her. Guys like this look for young, naive, inexperienced girls, usually girls with no siblings. They have a way of winning their confidence and belittling their parents, to the point the girls think this guy is the only one in the world who understands them and wants to see them become a star. It's an old story. Been done time and time again."

"How can we find out who he is? Where he might have taken her?" Mindy threw herself onto Bethany's bed, crying hysterically.

"It's doubtful he took her on public transportation. He probably drove." Captain Wyatt turned back to Lieutenant Terry. "Finding anything else in there that might be helpful?"

"Most of it is going over the same thing. Telling her how lucky he is to have found her. Emphasizing how excited her parents are going to be when she shows them the amount of money she'll make. He tells her she may want to buy her parents a big house in Beverly Hills so they can be close to her. It looks like she's told her diary nearly every conversation she's ever had with the guy."

Finding it almost impossible to breathe, Mindy gasped for air. "She'd never believe lies like those!"

"Oh, no!" Lieutenant Terry handed the diary to Captain Wyatt. "You'd better take a look at this."

He took it, read it for a moment, then gave

them a look Mindy would never forget as long as she lived. "In the last entry, the morning before she disappeared, she writes that she and her father had an argument because she was wearing too much lipstick and because he didn't like the shirt she had on and made her change it."

"I did," Chuck confessed, looking quickly toward Mindy. "It wasn't a real argument. I just insisted she take some of that lipstick off and change her shirt."

"She must have taken time to write in her diary when she came back into her bedroom. She says she was putting the shirt you complained about in her backpack so she could change back into it when she got to school."

Mindy glared at the captain. "Bethany would never go against her father's wishes like that!"

Lieutenant Terry held out the diary toward her. "Read it for yourself. She also told Trustworthy she wouldn't be able to talk to him on instant message that night because she'd be at play rehearsal until nine."

"You think this Trustworthy picked her up? I thought he lived in California!" Mindy said, trying to find her voice through her tears.

Lieutenant Terry latched on to Mindy's

hand. "Mrs. O'Connor, when you talk to someone on that instant-message thing, there is no way of knowing where that person actually is. They could tell you they were in Africa and be just a few miles from your home. You have to take their word they are telling you the truth."

"I'm going to contact a few people who have dealt with missing children and see if they've ever heard of Trustworthy." Captain Wyatt turned quickly to Lieutenant Terry. "When you're finished going through that diary, sign on to Bethany's computer. Run a search through Google and some of the other search engines for Trustworthy and see if anything comes up. It's a long shot, but it might be worth it. When you're finished, pull that hard drive out and bring it to the station. I've got a guy lined up who'll be able to check out the files and documents she deleted."

"Wait a minute!" Lieutenant Terry held the diary up in front of Captain Wyatt. "I found something else. An entry written several weeks ago. She says she lost the silver and turquoise bracelet he left for her in a box in the flowerbed in your front yard. The guy was right here! In Warren!"

Chuck and Mindy exchanged worried glances.

"We — we found that bracelet in the back-seat of our car," Chuck said with a sheepish look toward Mindy.

Mindy felt sick. Not only was her daughter missing, but now she knew she had falsely accused her husband of being with Michelle in the backseat of their car.

"Shouldn't we call the FBI or something?" Chuck asked, turning back to the officer.

Captain Wyatt moved toward the door. "I've already called them. An agent should be here anytime. Don't mention anything to the press or anyone else about anything, especially about the diary or what it says. If someone has taken your daughter, we don't want them to know we've found it. If any reporters call you, refer them to me. I'm going to set up that interview with the TV station; then we'll go over what you should say before it's videotaped. I'm sure they'll come to your house for the taping. I'll get back to you with a time."

Mindy and Chuck followed him as far as the family room. As soon as she heard the front door close, she rushed toward Chuck and wrapped her arms around his waist, unable to control her crying. "Can you ever forgive me? That bracelet didn't belong to Michelle! It was Bethany's!"

He nestled his chin in her hair. "I told you

that, but you wouldn't believe me."

She pressed her face against his chest and let the tears flow. "I know, and I'm so sorry."

Sliding the tip of his finger beneath her chin, he lifted her watery gaze to meet his. "I do love you, Mindy. You have to believe that. There's never been anyone but you."

"I want to believe you, but —" She leaned into him, loving the feel of his arms around her, the smell of his sweater, the touch of his fingers as they caressed her cheek. "I'm so tired, Chuck. So confused."

"I know, honey — so am I."

"Can we just forget about this Michelle thing until we find Bethany? I need you, Chuck. You've always been my fortress."

"I'm here for you, sweetheart. I'll always be here for you." Chuck took her hand and led her to the sofa.

She leaned back against the cushions and closed her eyes. "My eyes burn," she said in a half-whisper as drowsiness nearly overtook her.

"We both need sleep."

"But how can we sleep, knowing our daughter may be out there somewhere with a lunatic? Or maybe even worse — a child molester?"

Before he could answer, the cordless phone on the coffee table rang. Mindy snatched it up quickly. It was Janine.

"No, no word yet," Mindy told her.

"Is there anything else we can do? Jim wanted to go see one of his buddies in Providence today, but I refused to let him leave. I'm scared, Mindy. Is there anything else we can do to help? I told him while we were waiting for your call, he might as well paint the bedroom like I've been asking him. He's in there grumbling about it right now. If you need us, we can drop everything and give you a hand." She paused. "Oh, here's Jim. He wants to talk to Chuck. Can you put him on the phone?"

Mindy handed the phone to her husband. After a short conversation with the man, he hung up. "Both Jim and Janine said they are praying for Bethany's return."

The front door opened, and Captain Wyatt stepped in, holding one of his shoes in his hand. "You got any rags? Some dog left a pile in your front yard, and I stepped in it."

"Sure, out in the garage." Chuck stood and motioned the man to follow him. "There should be a bag of old rags on my workbench." He opened the door, flipped the light switch, and moved toward the opposite wall.

"Never mind. I see a rag hanging out of

144

this trash can. I just need something to wipe this smelly mess off my shoe. I was afraid it would stink up the whole squad car." Captain Wyatt grabbed the rag and began to wipe at his shoe. "Oh, oh!"

Chuck spun around, wondering what had caused his reaction.

CHAPTER EIGHT

"There's blood on this rag!"

"Blood?" Chuck leaned in for a better look. "I use that old shirt to wipe my hands when I change the oil in our cars, but there wasn't any blood on it, and I sure didn't put it in the trash."

"You're telling me this isn't your blood?"

"Captain Wyatt? The FBI agent is here," Mindy called out as she opened the door into the garage.

"Tell him he'd better come out here," the officer said, eyeing Chuck suspiciously.

A man with graying temples, wearing a dark sports coat and gray trousers, moved quickly into the garage. "I came as soon as I could. I'm Agent Cliff Rogers. You're Captain Wyatt?"

Captain Wyatt shifted the rag to his other hand. "Yes, and this is Chuck O'Connor, the father of the girl who is missing. I just made an interesting discovery. This rag was in the trash can. It has blood on it, and though Mr. O'Connor admits it's the one he uses when he changes the oil, he claims he didn't put it there and has no idea who did."

"I didn't put it there," Mindy said from her place in the doorway.

"How about your daughter?"

Chuck appeared thoughtful. "I can't remember the last time Bethany came out into the garage, except to get into the car. She never spends any time here."

The FBI agent reached out and took the rag. "Can you get me your daughter's hairbrush, ma'am? We'll need to check her DNA."

Chuck grabbed on to the man's arm. "You think that blood might be Bethany's?"

The man gave him a hard look as he pulled a plastic bag from the case he was carrying and slipped the rag into it. "We'll know when we check it."

With Captain Wyatt leading, the group moved back into the living room. After a short briefing, Agent Rogers questioned both Mindy and Chuck, taking notes and asking all sorts of questions that upset Mindy, personal questions about Bethany, which he explained had to be asked if they were to find her.

"I'll be honest with you," he said finally, closing his notebook. "The possibility of finding your daughter unharmed diminishes with each passing minute."

Shocked by the man's words, Chuck stood helplessly as Mindy went into hysterics. "Did you have to say that?" he asked angrily as he wrapped his arms around his wife. "She's about at the breaking point."

"I'm sorry, Mr. O'Connor, but you have to be prepared. I'm sure you've gone over things a dozen times, but you must do it again. Somewhere there has to be something that will give us a lead as to your daughter's whereabouts."

"You found out about Trustworthy! Isn't that enough?" Chuck snapped back, his own nerves shattering. "Are you working on that lead?"

"We're checking on that right now," Captain Wyatt said with a sympathetic look. "In addition to Lieutenant Terry, several top-notch computer experts are searching the Internet right now, looking for Trustworthy. The Center for Missing Children is going through their records, trying to find other girls who may have had contact with this person. Unfortunately, these guys usually change their nicknames with each new victim."

"Stop calling our daughter a victim!" Mindy shrieked at him.

"Look," Captain Wyatt said in a low, quiet voice. "You're both worn out. There's nothing more you can do tonight. The important thing right now is to get some sleep. Surely you have something in the medicine cabinet to help you relax. A number of people are working around the clock trying to find Bethany. Go to bed and try to sleep. You'll feel a lot better in the morning."

Chuck gave his wife's forehead a gentle kiss. "He's right, honey. Why don't we try to get some sleep? When Jim called, he said Bethany's Sunday school teacher, Treva Jordan, is at their house right now, and the three of them are calling all the volunteers and asking them to meet at the community center in the morning at nine. He suggested we fan the search out even farther and cover the outskirts of town. He's already drawn up another grid so we can make sure every property is covered."

With eyes so swollen she could barely see, Mindy let out a deep sigh. "You're probably right, but I'm not sure I'll be able to sleep, knowing our daughter is out there some—"

Chuck put a finger to her lips. "Don't even say it."

"You do need to sleep, dear." Mindy's

mother bent and patted her hand. "I doubt I'll sleep much either, but I am tired. I'm going on to bed. Let me know if you need me. Good night, everyone."

As soon as the officers and the FBI agent were out of the house, Chuck walked Mindy to their bedroom, kissing her good night in the doorway.

"Chuck?"

"Yes."

She gave him a demure smile that set his heart singing, despite the dreadful ordeal they were experiencing. "I — I don't want to sleep alone tonight. I need your arms around me."

Without a word Chuck swept her up in his arms and carried her into their room.

About three in the morning, he was awakened by Mindy tugging frantically on his arm.

"She called to me, Chuck! I heard her! Bethany was calling to me."

Even in the dim light from the moon, Chuck could tell his wife was smiling. "Go back to sleep, sweetheart. You must be dreaming."

She shook his arm even harder. "No, it wasn't a dream. I'm her mother! It was Bethany! I'm sure of it. She was calling out to me for help. She's alive, Chuck. I know she's alive!"

"Shh, shh." He pulled her to him and held her trembling body close, trying to calm her down.

Finally, the trembling stopped, and her breathing became almost normal. "Our baby is alive, Chuck," she said in a near whisper. "Bethany's alive."

Though they endured a troublesome night, with sleep coming in bits and snatches, both Mindy and Chuck crawled out of bed at six, feeling somewhat rested. He placed a call to Captain Wyatt, who told him there had been no further developments.

At exactly eight o'clock the doorbell rang. Mindy's mother hurried to answer it.

"My wife and I have been out of town. We just heard about Bethany," Pastor Bob Park explained as she motioned him inside. "We'd like to do anything we can to help. Bethany is very special to us. The ladies of our church are organizing a prayer chain."

Mindy's mother patted her daughter's arm. "I'll be in the kitchen if you need me. I'm going to put a roast in the oven."

Mindy nodded, then turned and gave the pastor a questioning look. "A prayer chain?"

"Within minutes of receiving a major

prayer request," he explained with a gentle smile, "our church ladies start calling the team prayer captains, who in turn call their assigned groups. Everyone drops what they're doing and goes to the Lord in prayer. Right now hundreds of our church members are praying for the safe return of your daughter."

"That's so sweet of them. Please thank them for us." Mindy swallowed at the lump in her throat, overwhelmed by the kindness and concern of people who did not even know them.

"I'd like to pray for her, too. Let's form a circle." Pastor Park reached out his hands, linking them with theirs, and lifted his face heavenward. "Lord, I come to You asking You to keep Bethany safe, wherever she is, and to return her to her home and to her parents and to those of us who love her. And be with whoever might be preventing her from coming home. Keep them from harming her in any way. She's Your child, God. She's accepted You as her Savior and turned her life over to You. And I ask You to be with Mindy and Chuck. They need Your touch of comfort, Lord. Speak to their hearts. Make Yourself real to them. We love You, God, and we ask these things in Jesus' name. Amen."

Mindy tried to hold in her emotions, but she couldn't. The pastor's words touched her in a way no words had ever before. She grabbed his arm, weeping so hard it was nearly impossible to form the words she wanted so much to say. "Oh, thank you, Pastor Park," she managed to get out finally. "I — I don't even know how to pray, and I'm not sure God would want to hear from me anyway."

The man put a comforting hand on her shoulder. "God is always ready to listen to His children, Mindy. Have you ever accepted Him as your Savior? Turned your life over to Him, the way Bethany has?"

"You know we've been attending church with her," Chuck said.

Pastor Park gave Chuck an understanding smile. "I know you have, Chuck, and you have no idea how much it means to Bethany to have you both there. But attending church doesn't make you a Christian. Getting right with God does. Your daughter has been concerned about both of you. She has been praying for your salvation."

"We've heard your messages on sin, but we've never thought of ourselves as sinners," Chuck said defensively.

The ringing of the phone put an end to their conversation. It was Jim Porter telling

153

them the volunteers had all been briefed and given their assignments.

"We'll be right there." Chuck punched the OFF button on the phone. "Jim said it might help if we came over and talked to the volunteers before they left."

"I'll go with you," Pastor Park said. "I want to help."

By three o'clock all of the volunteers had returned, but most had little to report. A few had been told about a blue van several had seen cruising through one of the neighborhoods; some mentioned a man on a motorcycle who had been riding up and down a side street, making lewd comments to anyone who would listen. But other than that no one reported anything out of the ordinary.

Agent Rogers arrived at their house about the same time Mindy and Chuck turned into their driveway. "I've brought some pictures. I'd like you both to take a look at them. See if any of them look familiar." He followed them into the house and placed the big book on the coffee table. "Take your time. If you see anyone the least bit familiar, let me know."

"Who are these men?" Mindy asked as she

and Chuck sat down and stared at the first page.

"Child molesters."

Mindy's breathing quickened, and she had a difficult time swallowing.

"These guys move from place to place. Maybe one of them came to your door posing as a salesman, a repairman, something of that sort. Or maybe you saw him around Bethany's school. Sometimes they just sit in their cars and watch until they find a likely victim."

With a frown Chuck held up his flattened palm. "I've asked you not to use that word. It upsets my wife."

"Sorry, but that's exactly what these men do."

"Why aren't they in prison?" Mindy asked, gazing at the pictures.

"Most of them have already served time, and they're either out on parole or have been released," he answered matter-of-factly. "There's no way to keep them off the streets or from doing the same thing again."

Nearly an hour later Chuck closed the book and handed it back to Agent Rogers. "Sorry. Neither of us recognized anyone."

When the phone rang, both Mindy and Chuck grabbed for it, hoping it was good news, but it was only a reporter from a tabloid trying to get an exclusive interview.

Agent Rogers set up shop in the little den Chuck used as his home office, leaving Mindy and Chuck alone in the family room.

"Mindy, I've been thinking about what Pastor Park said — you know — when he asked us if we'd ever accepted Christ as our Savior, the way Bethany did." Holding on to the cup of coffee his mother-in-law had brought to him, he crossed the room and sat down by his wife. "Did you hear the way that man prayed? It was as if he was having a conversation with God Himself. I half-expected God to answer him right then and there."

Mindy, cradling a framed picture of her daughter, nodded. "I know what you mean. That's the way Bethany prays when I tuck her in at night. I — I wish —" She stopped and stared at her daughter's image.

"I know. I loved to hear her pray, too, but I figured God really didn't care about the prayer of a child. I" — he gave her a hang-dog grin — "I guess I always thought praying was something preachers did, not kids."

Mindy dabbed at her reddened nose again. "I hate to admit it, but when Bethany would talk to me about becoming a Christian, I actually made fun of her."

"I guess I did, too. Now I wish I had her

faith." Chuck smiled as he remembered several conversations he'd had with his daughter about that very thing. "She tried to convince me that all people were sinners and needed to go to God and ask Him for forgiveness, then turn their lives over to Him. I scoffed at her words. Now I'm ashamed of myself." He sat staring at the photograph in his wife's hands. "I wish I would have listened to her."

"She told me I was a sinner, too, but because of my silly pride, I scolded her for talking about me that way." Mindy turned to face him, and he could see the hurt in her eyes as a tear made its way down her cheek. "I — I wish we'd asked Pastor Park to show us how to become Christians. I want that kind of faith, Chuck. I need it! I want to be able to call out to God and know I'm His child. I just don't know how."

"He said to call him if there was anything he could do for us." Chuck picked up the remote phone from the coffee table. "Shall I call him? I'm sure he'd come right back."

Desperate to ease the pain of her loss, Mindy lowered her head and pressed the photograph to her heart. "Yes, Chuck, call him."

Pastor Park rang their doorbell a half hour later.

"You didn't say why you wanted me to come," he said as he rushed into the room. "Have you heard anything about Bethany?"

"No, Pastor Park, no news, but that's not why I called you." He turned to Mindy with a smile. "My precious wife and I are ready to become Christians. We're tired of playing church on Sunday mornings. We want the real thing. Like our daughter has."

"That's the best news I've heard in weeks. Bethany has been praying for your salvation. She never lost faith that this would happen."

"Mindy and I have discussed this at length. We want the same kind of faith Bethany has, and we're willing to do whatever it takes to get it."

Giving them each a warm smile, Pastor Park sat down between them and opened his Bible. After reading and explaining a number of Scripture passages, he asked, "Are you sure you understand what it means to become a Christian? You're not going to be suddenly perfect, with everything going exactly the way you'd like it to — believe me, it won't work like that. But as a child of God, if you let Him and want His perfect will for your life, He'll take control. Remember — God has promised never to leave or forsake His children." He closed his Bible, placing it on the table in front of them. "Are you ready to make that decision?"

"Yes, Pastor, we are." Chuck stood and, crossing over to Mindy, reached for her hand, then knelt beside the sofa, pulling his wife down beside him.

"Then pray with me," Pastor Park said, placing a hand on each head.

When he finished praying for both Chuck and Mindy, he prayed for Bethany's safe return. Somehow, hearing Pastor Park pray so fervently for their child gave Chuck new hope. "Thank you, Pastor Park. We're very grateful to you for being so good to our Bethany and for coming over like this."

Pastor Park slipped an arm around Mindy as they all stood. "Have faith in God. You're in His hands. Whatever happens, you must accept as His will for your life. To draw close to Him, read your Bible and pray." He gave them a grin. "And attend our church every Sunday." Then with an outright laugh he added, "That last part wasn't from the scriptures. I added that one. We love seeing the O'Connor family lined up in the pew on Sundays."

Chuck, along with Mindy, walked Pastor Park to the door, once again thanking him for coming and for treating them in such a loving way.

"Well, we did it!" Chuck said, grabbing Mindy up and whirling her about the room.

Mindy threw her arms around his neck and held on fast. "We did, didn't we? Oh, Chuck, I feel really good about what we have done. I've wanted so much to pray for our daughter's safe return, but honestly I didn't think God would want to hear from me. I've turned my back on Him all these years, feeling totally self-sufficient. Who did I think I was?"

"I was the same way." He stopped whirling and set her down on her feet. "Maybe if we'd done this a long time ago, when we were first married, we could have spared ourselves all those troubled years when we would only fight and disagree." He tightened his grip around her waist and stared lovingly into her eyes. "I know you still have misgivings about Michelle and me, and you have every right to. I haven't been able to prove my innocence yet, sweetheart." He paused and lifted the flat of his palm to her. "As our God is my witness, I never did anything indecent with that woman. Just trust me. Please — trust me."

Mindy stared up at him, her eyes misting over. She wanted so much to believe him;

but she still had too many unanswered questions, and right now her focus had to be on finding Bethany. She did not have the will or the strength to deal with the Michelle thing at this moment. "I want to trust you, Chuck. You mean everything to me, but —" She bit her lip, choosing her words carefully. "Let's forget about that woman for now and pretend she never existed, and then we'll deal with your suspension after we find our daughter." She stood on tiptoe and gently kissed his lips. "I promise I'll help prove your innocence in any way I can."

"You mean it? You'll help me?"

"Yes. I want to help you, Chuck." *Even if it means going Dumpster-diving again!*

Chuck glanced at his watch. "I had no idea it was so late. The TV crew will be here in an hour."

Mindy turned toward the clock on the wall. "I was going to put a load in the washer, and then I want to freshen up."

He nodded. "I need to take a quick shower, but first I'm going to jot down a few things I want to make sure we cover when we do the interview."

Mindy had barely left the room when the phone rang.

"I'm glad I caught you, Chuck," a male voice said on the other end.

Chuck pressed the phone tightly to his ear. "Hello, Jake."

"I spoke with your mother-in-law last night, and she told me you'd had no further word about your daughter's disappearance. I'm so sorry, Chuck. I wish I could do something to help."

"Thanks, Jake. There seems to be nothing anyone can do. This waiting is terrible." Chuck rotated his stiff neck.

"Well, I may not be able to do anything about finding your daughter, but I do have good news. I fired Michelle this morning."

Chuck sucked in a deep breath and held it, afraid he'd misunderstood his boss's words. "Does that mean —"

"It means you have your job back, and I owe you an apology."

"You have no idea how glad I am to hear you say that. But why? How?"

"From the glowing reference her former boss, Alexander Delmar, of the huge Florida-based Delmar Industries gave her, I had no reason to feel otherwise, but I thought it might be worthwhile to call Mr. Delmar. I wanted to ask him about Michelle's former work record and see if perhaps there had been any problems with her we hadn't heard about. I've been trying to phone that man for over two weeks but was told he was on his annual African safari and unable to be reached until he returned. Today was the first day he was back in his office, and after the hard time I gave his secretary by calling her nearly every day, she put me through to him."

Beads of perspiration broke out across Chuck's forehead as he sat down on a nearby chair. "What — what did he have to say?"

"At first the man was reluctant to talk to me, but I explained that my best salesman's reputation was at stake and I needed any information he could give me."

Chuck's heart pounded wildly. Dare he hope Jake had discovered something about Michelle?

"Finally, after I explained about the charges Michelle had filed against you and how I'd had no choice but to put you on suspension, he began to open up. He asked me about your work record and how well I knew you. I could tell the man was not being completely honest with me, so I told him about Bethany's disappearance and the horrible time you and Mindy were having waiting, with no word of her whereabouts."

Jake nervously cleared his throat. "Chuck, she did it there, too. In Florida. Only that time Mr. Delmar was the victim."

Chuck straightened in his chair, shocked by Jake's words. "You mean she falsely accused him of the same thing she did me?"

"Yes, but he asked me to keep it quiet. It seems Michelle played on his sympathies just as she did you, asking him to drive her home, taking him out for dinner, inviting him to a sold-out NCAA game because she had two tickets that were going to go to waste unless she could find someone to go with her, and other things, too. Even called him saying she was afraid someone was trying to break into her apartment. His words sounded like a carbon copy of what you'd told me. Finally, she made her play for him, and like you he turned her down. The next day she showed up in his office, threatening to accuse him of raping her if he didn't give her a good severance package, which he considered as a payoff, and an excellent letter of reference. He said he hated to do it, but he knew what an accusation like that could do to his marriage, his reputation, and his business, so he did it. He hoped meeting her demands would put an end to it all."

"Amazing," was all Chuck could say.

"The poor man said he hasn't had a good night's sleep since the day she walked out of his office. The guilt of letting her get away with her lecherous scheme has nearly ruined his life. He's been consumed with the possibility she'd do the same thing to someone else. And unfortunately she did. To you."

"I — I don't know what to say. I was so afraid I wouldn't be able to prove my innocence. You have no idea how happy this makes me, Jake."

"As I said, Chuck, I owe you an apology. I only hope you can understand why I had to suspend you until this thing was cleared up. I intend to do everything I can to make things right. You've not only been the best salesman I've ever had, but you've also been a good friend. I — I hope we can continue to be friends."

"Who is it, Chuck?" Mindy asked, hurrying into the room with an armful of freshly laundered towels.

Chuck couldn't hold back the wide smile that erupted across his face. "It's Jake," he told her, covering the mouthpiece. "It's over, sweetheart. I have my old job back! I'll tell you all about it as soon as I finish talking to him."

Setting aside her load, Mindy dropped down beside him, smiling as she placed her arm around his shoulders and gave him a squeeze.

"I don't expect you to come back to work

now, Chuck," Jake went on, "but I am anxious to meet with you. I said you had your old job back. That's not quite true."

Chuck's heart sank.

"I've hired another man to fill your job."

"But you —"

"Hear me out, Chuck. I hired that man because I'm making you sales manager. I hope you'll accept the position, because you've earned it. There's not another person who deserves it more. Of course you'll have a substantial increase in pay, a nice office, and a number of other perks."

Chuck had cried only three times in his adult life: when his mother found out she had cancer, when Jake put him on suspension and Mindy asked him to move into the guest room, and when they realized their precious Bethany was missing. Tears filled his eyes now and ran down his cheeks as he cradled the phone in his hands. "Accept the position? Of course I'll accept it. I've looked forward to being sales manager since the first day I came to work for you."

Chuck slipped an arm around Mindy and pulled her close. "Thanks, Jake. Thanks for everything, and thanks for believing in me and going to all that effort. I owe you."

"You owe me nothing, Chuck. It's a pleasure to help and promote a man like you. I won't keep you. I'll be praying for you and Mindy and the safe return of Bethany. Keep me posted and let me know if there is anything I can do."

Chuck rested his cheek against Mindy's. "I will, Jake, and thanks again."

Mindy gazed into his eyes. "Oh, Chuck, this is the best news we've had in a long time. Did I understand it right? Jake gave you a promotion?"

Feeling he almost needed to pinch himself to make sure he wasn't dreaming, Chuck planted a kiss on Mindy's cheek, then smiled at her. "Yes, he did. Mindy, my love, you're looking at the new sales manager. Our prayers about my suspension have been answered." He rose, pulling her up with him, feeling more encouraged than he had in a long time. "Maybe God will answer our prayers about our daughter, too. Let's get ready for the interview!"

Though Chuck was fairly successful at fighting back tears, Mindy wept openly throughout the entire interview.

"I'm sorry," she told the reporter as he and the videographer packed up to leave. "I had promised myself I wouldn't cry like that, but I'm so concerned about Bethany that I couldn't help it."

The reporter placed his hand on her arm and gave her an understanding smile. "Of course you cried. I'm sure my mom would have cried, too, if I'd been missing. Moms do that. You did fine. I just hope this interview will bring your daughter back to you. Maybe someone in our viewing audience will have the lead you're looking for."

She and Chuck thanked the two young men. But even before their news cruiser was out of sight, Captain Wyatt's squad car pulled into the drive, and he and Agent Rogers stepped out. From the look on their faces, it was obvious they were the bearers of bad news.

CHAPTER NINE

"We're going to have to ask you to come with us," Captain Wyatt said firmly as he took Chuck by the arm.

"Why?" Mindy screamed out, grabbing on and clinging to her husband's hand. "What's happened? Have you found Bethany? You have to tell us!"

"No, ma'am," the captain replied, his face void of expression. "I'm sorry. We've had no further news of your daughter's whereabouts."

"What's going on here?" Mrs. Carson asked as she came in from the kitchen. "Why are you holding on to my son-in-law's arm like that?"

Captain Wyatt motioned her aside with a nod of his head. "Just step back, ma'am."

"Where are you taking me, and why?" Chuck asked as he struggled to pull his arm free.

Agent Rogers took over. "The blood on

the rag found in your garage matches your daughter's DNA. We're taking you to the station for further questioning."

"I'm coming with you," Mindy said resolutely as she headed for the closet to get her jacket.

"No, you stay here. I'm sure I'll be back soon. I have no idea how Bethany's blood got on that rag." Chuck gave Mindy a tender smile. "Please, Mindy, stay here with your mother. Pray they'll find our daughter and this nightmare will end."

It broke her heart to see her husband being herded off to the police station like some criminal, and as soon as the squad car was out of the driveway, Mindy dropped to her knees and began to pray.

Two hours later Chuck returned, looking exhausted.

"What did they do to you?" Mindy asked, rushing to him as the door closed behind him. "You look awful!"

He circled her waist with his long arms and rubbed his cheek against hers. "They all but accused me of having something to do with our daughter's disappearance. I think they're clutching at straws since they haven't been able to find any other evidence."

"You'd never harm Bethany!"

"You know that, but they don't. To them I'm a suspect, the only one they've been able to turn up. I told them I had no idea why her blood would be on that rag, but since it was one of the rags I use in the garage, they don't believe me."

"Oh, Chuck, this is too much. I've been praying almost all the time you've been gone."

He cradled her head in his hand and pressed it to his chest. "We have to have faith, sweetheart. Remember what Pastor Park said? God has promised never to leave us or forsake us. We have to trust Him to take care of our little girl, wherever she is, and bring her back to us."

At ten that evening the two sat huddled in front of the TV set, watching the interview they'd taped that very day. It ended with a plea directly to the audience from Mindy as she held Bethany's picture to her breast. Chuck turned off the TV, then reached out and took his wife's hand in his. "Honey, no one could resist that plea. If anyone knows anything, I'm sure they'll call the authorities."

Mindy leaned against him, absorbing his strength. "I know wherever our daughter is — with her strong faith in God — she's praying, too. Probably for us. She knows how much we love her."

"She also knows we won't quit until we find her. We have to be strong for her sake."

The interview generated hundreds of phone calls to the command center that had been set up in the community building, but none of them seemed promising enough to offer much hope of finding her or her abductor.

Three more long, arduous days went by, with still no clues as to Bethany's whereabouts. Chuck had watched Mindy cry and cry, until there seemed to be no more tears for her to shed. Her stomach ached, her head hurt, and she said every bone in her body felt as if it were on fire.

She had not mentioned it to him, but he knew in his heart that this was the day his wife had been dreading.

Mother's Day.

Mindy smiled at him as she came out of their bedroom, dressed and ready for the day. Despite the lack of sleep and the dark circles under her eyes, she was beautiful. He had tried to be a rock to her through all of this, hoping his displays of love and devotion would make it hard for her even to consider that he'd had anything to do with Michelle.

Moving quickly to her side, he took both

her hands in his and lifted them to his lips, kissing them as he gazed into her swollen, watery eyes.

"You don't need to avoid mentioning it, Chuck. I know it's Mother's Day. I'm just hoping and praying this will be the day Bethany comes home to us."

"Bethany couldn't have asked for a better mother, sweetheart. Just remember that." He slipped an arm around her. "Let's go to the Center. We have work to do."

To their surprise, despite its being Mother's Day, the day most folks spend with their families, a number of volunteers were already at the Warren Community Center when they arrived. After greeting everyone and thanking them for their diligence in helping them look for Bethany, Chuck moved to the big gridded map on the wall, gazing at the hundreds of colored ball-headed pins the many volunteers had placed there to show the houses and buildings they had canvassed. He carefully scanned each area that had been covered. "Hey, Jim," he called out when he checked an area at the extreme lower end of the grid. "Why hasn't this area down here by Bristol been covered? There isn't a single pin in it."

Jim Porter placed a stack of papers on the table and hurried over to him. "Hey, don't

173

worry about that area. I know it very well. Me and a buddy of mine have hunted and fished there a number of times. Take it from me. Sending the volunteers down there would only be a waste of time. I think we'd be better off having them backtrack some of the areas where they've already been." He rushed off to answer one of the many ringing phones.

Treva Jordan moved up beside Chuck as he continued to gaze at the map. "I was raised in that area, Chuck. I just assumed it had been searched. My aunt's in a care home in Bristol, but she still owns a house there. I remember a number of old, abandoned outbuildings and barns not too far from her. She even has two or three on her place. Want me to take a couple of the volunteers and go down there?"

Chuck nodded as his index finger traced the edges of the uncanvassed portion on the map. "That's a great idea, but I can't ask these people to give up the entire day. It's Mother's Day. I have a better idea. I'll go with you. We'll get two or three other people to go with us."

"How about Jim?" Treva asked. "He seems to want to be in on everything that's going on."

Chuck glanced toward the table where Jim

was sorting out a new batch of flyers and shook his head. "No, let's give him a rest. He and Janine have been working way too many hours on this. Don't even mention it to him, or he'll want to go."

"Did I hear you say you were going to search the area around Bristol?"

Chuck recognized the voice. "Hey, Pastor Park. What are you doing here on a Sunday morning? Aren't you supposed to be at church?"

"It appears both Treva and I are playing hooky today." The pastor nudged Treva's arm, then gave Chuck's hand a warm shake. "Normally I would be, but we have a special speaker this morning to commemorate Mother's Day. A woman from our congregation who has quite a story to tell. I left things in her capable hands. I've taken practically no vacation time in the past few years, so I told our church board I wanted today and tomorrow off so I could help you and Mindy. I'd like to go to Bristol with you. I've held some evangelistic meetings there, so I'm fairly familiar with that area. My wife is here, too. I'm sure she'd like to come along. We can take my Durango."

Chuck gave him a grateful smile. "I'd be mighty happy to have you both along, Pastor."

"I heard you. I'm going, too."

Turning, Chuck faced a look of determination on Mindy's face. "You need to stay here, sweetheart. You're worn out. You can drive our car on home."

Mindy held on tightly to his arm. "I'm going with you."

He could tell by the set of her jaw that there was no way he could discourage her. "Okay, that makes five of us. Let me get one of the single men to go along, and we'll be on our way."

Even after five hours of searching abandoned buildings and talking to local residents, nothing new turned up. Standing before the tired, hungry group, Chuck pulled off his cap and ran his hands through his hair. "I guess Jim Porter was right. Maybe we'd better give up and head back to Warren."

"But we haven't checked out my aunt's place yet," Treva said. "It's only about a mile from here."

Mindy tugged on his arm. "We're already here. Let's check it out, Chuck."

He cupped his wife's chin with his hand. "You sure? It's been a long day already."

She sent him a weak smile. "Yes, I'm sure."

■ ■ ■ ■

"I'd never say this to anyone but you, Pastor," Chuck said in a low voice as they pulled into the yard of the house owned by Treva's aunt and the two men climbed out of the vehicle. "I've spent quite a bit of time on the Missing Children's Web site, and from what I've read we have very little chance of finding our daughter alive."

"Chuck, don't give up hope!" The pastor placed his hand on Chuck's shoulder.

"I'm not, Pastor Park, but I have to face the possibility."

"I understand what you're saying, Chuck, but let's not give up hope yet. God is able."

"Treva and I are going to check out the house," Mindy told her husband as she crawled out of the backseat and pulled her scarf up around her neck. "She knows where the key is hidden."

"Just be careful," he called after her. "And don't take too long. We need to head back to Warren." After sending Pastor Park and his wife off to the west to check out a shed Treva had told them about, he and Cal Rivers, the single man he'd asked to come with them, headed off toward the old, dilapidated barn out behind the house.

Their search of the old barn yielded nothing more than a few broken gallon jugs, a ball of heavy twine, and a couple of rotten wooden crates. "Nobody's been here in years," Chuck said, brushing his hands on his jeans. "This is a beautiful piece of property, but the buildings sure aren't much. I hope the house is in better shape. Let's walk on toward the east a couple hundred more yards; then we'll head for the Durango."

Treva and Mindy arrived back at the vehicle minutes after the men got there. "Nothing in the house, but you should see the view of the bay from there. It's beautiful!" Mindy told him as she crawled in beside him. "Aren't the Parks back yet?"

"No, not yet."

"I'm so sorry you're having to do this on Mother's Day," Mindy told Cal and Treva, holding back her tears. "You should be home with your families on a day like this."

"I love that daughter of yours," Treva said. "She's very special to me. I was there when Pastor Park led her to the Lord."

Mindy's brows raised. "I didn't know that!"

"Mindy and I finally accepted the Lord," Chuck said with a big smile. "We're so anxious to tell Bethany about it. Pastor Park led us to the Lord, too, just like he led her."

"That news is going to make your daughter one happy girl." Treva's voice was filled with excitement. "She's really been praying for the two of you, and she had faith that God would answer her prayer."

"You know her well, Treva. Do you think Bethany would go away with someone she didn't know?"

Treva's eyes rounded. "Bethany? Never, Mindy! That girl has a good head on her shoulders."

Mindy let out a relieved sigh. "That's what I was hoping you'd say."

"What could be taking them so long?" Chuck scanned the area off to the west. "I'm going to go find them. We need to get back." He pushed the door open and crawled out.

Suddenly Pastor Park's voice rang out from a dense grove of trees about a hundred yards from where they were parked. "Chuck! Mindy! Come over here, quick!"

CHAPTER TEN

"Is it Bethany?" Chuck screamed out, racing toward the pastor's voice. "Is she alive?"

"I can't tell!" he called back. "Hurry!"

Chuck ran as fast as he could, pushing his way through thick boughs and overgrowth, his heart pounding with both joy and fear. "She has to be alive!"

"Look through this crack!" Pastor Park yelled out excitedly as he pointed to a separation between two weathered boards in the old shed. "I can see her! She's under that pile of dirty old horse blankets. You can barely see her face!"

Chuck squinted his eyes and peered through. "It's her. Oh, dear God, it's her! You've answered our prayer!" He tugged on the padlock securing the door, but it would not give.

"I'll get my tire iron." Pastor Park hurried away toward the Durango.

"Oh, Chuck, is it really her?" Panting for

breath, Mindy reached for his arm. "Is — is she alive?"

"I — I don't know." He shoved her toward the space between the two boards. "Take a look. Can you tell if she's breathing?"

Mindy pressed her face against the opening. "Bethany, baby, Mama and Daddy are here! Can you hear me? Oh, baby, please say something!"

Pastor Park tossed the tire iron into Chuck's hand. "Here — try this."

Chuck shoved the tip of the tire iron under the hasp and gave it a sharp yank. It budged slightly but did not open. He tried it a second time and the hasp gave way. He jerked open the door and rushed to Bethany, dropping onto his knees at her side, bending and listening for any signs of life.

"Oh, Chuck, we've found her!" Mindy screamed as she threw herself down beside Bethany and began to stroke her beloved child's hair. "Oh, thank You, God! Thank You! This is the best Mother's Day present I could ever ask for!"

"She's breathing, but barely, and she has a nasty cut on her head." Chuck pulled off his jacket and threw it on top of the blankets covering the still, small body curled up on the dirt floor of the shed. "We've got to get her to the hospital."

Cal bent down and began to take the girl's pulse. "I've already used my cell phone to call for an ambulance. They should be here shortly. She may not have had food," he added, looking around, "but she had water, thanks to that hole in the roof. Looks like that rain we had a few days ago must've run right off that roof into this old bucket."

Slowly Bethany opened one eye and peered out through the slit. "Daddy?" she whispered faintly.

He shot a smile to his wife. "I'm here, Princess. So is Mommy." Carefully Chuck slipped his hand beneath her shoulders, bracing her head with his arm. "You're safe now."

The girl simply nodded as her eyes closed again.

"We're going to take you home, sweetheart," Mindy told her, her fingers stroking the girl's matted hair. "You're going to be just fine."

Chuck silently thanked God as he heard the wail of the ambulance's siren. *Lord, I know I don't deserve it, but thank You for answering this father's prayer.*

After examining her, the EMTs agreed to take her back to Warren, which was only a five-mile trip, instead of into Bristol. Chuck and Mindy were allowed to ride to the hospital with their daughter.

Chuck glanced impatiently at his watch as he and Mindy sat in the hospital's waiting room. "What's taking so long? She's been in there for nearly two hours."

Mindy crossed her arms over her chest and leaned back in the chair. "I don't know, but I think we should be with her. I know she's still terrified."

Agent Rogers rose to his feet and began to pace around the waiting room. "I don't want to frighten you, Mr. and Mrs. O'Connor, but Bethany is still in grave danger. She's the only one who can identify the person who did this to her." He pushed one of the upholstered chairs in front of them and sat down. "I've placed one of my best men here at the hospital to guard her room. We don't want to take any chances."

Mindy's hand went to her chest. "You think he'd actually come here? To the hospital?"

"We don't know, but until we find whoever it was who kidnapped your daughter, we have to take as many precautions as possible."

"Your daughter has been through a terrible ordeal," the doctor told Mindy and Chuck as he stepped into the waiting room. "I doubt she's had any food. She's been exposed to the cold, even though I've heard her abductor did leave some old horse blankets for her, and it appears she's been either hit or shoved into something. She has a broken rib and bruises over her entire body."

Mindy let out a gasp and buried her head against Chuck's chest. "Oh, no, not my baby!"

Chuck knew what his wife was thinking. Though they had never voiced it to each other, it had been his worse fear, too. "Was she —"

"Raped? No."

Chuck could not help it. He burst into tears right along with Mindy. "Praise You, Lord!"

The doctor placed a comforting hand on Mindy's shoulder. "She's going to be sore for a while, but give her a little time, some good food, and a lot of love, and she'll be fine. I've already stitched up that cut on her head. She wants to see you. But don't expect too much. She's still in a bit of a stupor and maybe will be for some time to come. It may be several days, maybe even weeks, before she's more like her old self, and even then she'll no doubt have night-mares. In fact, she may not want to sleep at all. More than likely she hasn't slept since she was taken. I've given her something to sleep, so we'd better hurry if you want to talk to her before she drifts off."

"Has — has she said anything about what happened to her?"

"No, Mrs. O'Connor," the doctor said, with a glance toward Agent Rogers. "Nothing. I doubt she'll want to talk about it. Victims seldom do. Now follow me. I'll take you to her."

Mindy and Chuck moved quietly up to Bethany's bed.

"Baby, are you awake?" Mindy whispered, bending over to stroke her daughter's cheek. "It's Mama. Daddy's here, too."

Slowly Bethany opened her eyes and gazed at them, squinting and blinking as if she were having trouble focusing.

"We love you, Princess," Chuck said, smiling at his daughter. "And we have something to tell you."

Mindy bent and kissed her daughter's cheek. "Treva told us you'd been praying for us, that we'd accept God like you had."

"We did it, sweetheart. Your mama and me. We accepted Christ as our Savior."

"Pastor Park helped us. He led us to your Lord."

Bethany opened one eye as a smile took

birth on her dry, chapped lips. "Really?" she said faintly.

Chuck nodded. "Really. We'll talk more about it later. There's so much we want to tell you. Right now you need to rest."

They hadn't noticed that Agent Rogers had followed them into the room. "Ask her who did this to her."

Chuck nodded at the man and leaned in closer. "Who took you from us, Bethany? Can you tell Daddy?"

Bethany turned her head away, and her entire body began to shake violently. "No! Leave me alone!" she shouted, her eyes widening and taking on a glassy glaze. "Don't let him hurt me! Please — don't let him hurt me again!"

"You'll have to leave," the doctor said firmly, motioning them toward the door. "This child has had a terrible shock. I won't have her upset." He ushered them out of the room, with all three protesting.

"She's my daughter!" Mindy nearly screamed at him, refusing to be separated from Bethany. "I have to be with her!"

"Once she's asleep," he told them, his voice now kind and gentle, "if you promise you won't upset her, you can stay in the room with her — but no more questions tonight. Understood?"

Agent Rogers whipped out his badge and presented it to the man. "We're talking a kidnapping here. The person who did this is still out there, running loose, maybe already planning to kidnap some other child. I need answers."

The doctor stepped forward and stood nose to nose with the agent. "And you'll get them, but not until that child is ready to talk to you. I'm sorry, Agent Whatever-Your-Name-Is, but the health of the little girl comes first. Right now she needs rest."

"I think one of us should be with Bethany at all times," Mindy told Chuck. "I'd like to stay with her tonight. You go on home and get some rest. Maybe by morning she'll feel like talking to us. I don't even care if she knows I'm in the room. I just want to sit and watch her breathe."

"I should be the one to stay. You're exhausted. You go —"

"Please, Chuck, it's Mother's Day. Let me spend the rest of it with my daughter."

Chuck smiled as he nodded his head. "Okay, sweetheart, you stay. I'll come back first thing in the morning."

The doctor reached out to Chuck's arm. "I'm sorry. I didn't mean to sound harsh. I know both you and your wife want to stay with your daughter. I have a daughter of my own. I'll permit it if you promise not to ask her any more questions. I'm sure you understand why."

Chuck's heart did a leap at the news. He hated the idea of having to leave. "We can both stay?"

"Yes. Just remember my words. I'll be checking on her the first thing in the morning."

The two sat quietly, holding hands and watching the rhythmic rise and fall of Bethany's chest. About two in the morning, Chuck stood to his feet and stretched. "Want to go with me to see if we can find a vending machine? I'm thirsty." He was glad when she nodded and reached out her hand.

"Good evening. I'm Officer Kirkpatrick."

Mindy startled as she stepped into the hall, having forgotten about the guard posted by the door.

"Oh! Hello. We're Bethany's parents."

"Got any idea where the vending machines are?" Chuck asked the man after shaking his hand.

Before the officer could answer, a nurse called out to them from the nurses' station. "Mr. and Mrs. O'Connor. There's a bag over here for you and your wife. A man, I think his name was Park or Parks, left it for you. He said he knew you and your wife hadn't eaten all day, and he brought you some sandwiches and some other things. There's a small lunchroom and a coffee machine at the end of the hall."

Chuck hurried to retrieve the bag; then he and Mindy made their way toward the lunchroom. "Good old Pastor Park. What a thoughtful guy."

"God really answers prayer. The way he kept Bethany alive and the way He led us to her — now this! Food when we really need it."

"Mr. O'Connor!"

Both Chuck and Mindy turned as a man stepped up beside them.

"I'm Bill Dayton from WBBB radio. I wondered if I might ask you a few questions. I know your daughter was found somewhere not far from here." He went on without giving Chuck time to answer. "Can you tell me where and who did this to her?"

Chuck shook his head and gave him a menacing stare. "I think you'd better talk to Captain Wyatt or Agent Rogers about that."

"I couldn't help overhearing Mrs. O'Connor make some comment about God answering your prayers. You really don't think God had anything to do with your finding her, do you?"

Chuck glanced at Mindy, then squared

his shoulders. "Yes, I do. My wife and I are both Christians now, and we believe in prayer. We're confident God took care of our daughter while she was away from us and led us to find her."

The man gave him a mocking frown. "If I were a Christian, which I'm not, I would be furious with God for letting something like this happen to one of my family members. Are you telling me this tragic kidnapping didn't shake your faith in God?"

Chuck silently sent up a quick prayer. *Let me answer this man in a way that will honor You!* "No, not at all. I can honestly say that finding our daughter has deepened our faith in God. I feel sad for you if you don't know Him and would suggest you get yourself right with Him. If you'd like, I'd be happy to provide a Bible for you."

"Ah — thanks for your time. I'll check with the police." The man nearly tripped over his feet getting out the door.

"You were wonderful," Mindy said, smiling up at Chuck, her weary eyes now sparkling. "I'm so proud of you." She giggled as she gave his arm a pinch. "For a brand-new Christian you did very well."

Her melodic giggle made him smile. What a joy to see his wife happy again. Even the worry lines on her face had begun to relax.

He playfully tapped the tip of her nose with his index finger. "Only because I sent up a prayer to God, asking Him to give me the right words."

Bethany struggled to open her eyes. Why hadn't they left a light on? She hated the darkness. *Oh, I hurt.* Painfully she shifted her weight a bit, turning toward the two empty chairs beside her bed. *Mama! Daddy! Where are you?*

Carefully she rolled onto her back, wincing at the stifling pain in her chest from the broken rib. *Mama! Daddy! Come back. I don't want to be alone. Please come back!*

She stared at the narrow shaft of light wedging its way through the nearly closed door as it suddenly widened and the silhouette of a man appeared.

"Daddy, is that you? Where's Mama?"

But her father didn't answer.

"Daddy?"

CHAPTER ELEVEN

The figure closed the door, rendering the room in near darkness again. Though he was not nearly as visible now, with only the light filtering in through the closed Venetian blinds, she could still see him as he crept stealthily toward the bed.

That's not my daddy!

Panic gripped her heart as the experiences of the last few days flooded her mind and soul. *Is it him? The man who kidnapped me?* She wanted to scream out, to yell for help, but the words were trapped in her throat and would not come.

As he moved closer, instinctively, with trembling fingers, she grabbed the sheet and pulled it tightly around her neck, her heart clenching with fear and pounding so loudly she was sure he could hear it. She tried to back away as his hot breath scorched her cheek, but it was impossible.

There was no place to run.

No way to escape.

Mindy took Chuck's hand as they made their way toward Bethany's room after they had consumed the delicious sandwiches and pieces of cake Pastor Park had brought. "I'm so glad the doctor said we could both stay the night with her."

Chuck gave her a doting smile as they came to Bethany's room. He reached for the door handle, then pulled back. "Where's the guard?"

A blood-curdling scream sounded from the room!

Chuck rushed in, momentarily blinded by the semi-darkness. Someone was leaning over Bethany! "Get help!" he yelled at Mindy as he hurled himself at the figure, grabbing the person around the shoulders and wrestling whoever it was to the floor.

"Help! Someone, help!" Mindy yelled at the top of her lungs.

Instantly two orderlies appeared and rushed through the door. With their help Chuck was able to subdue the man.

"Jim!" He couldn't believe his eyes. It was Jim Porter, the man he had thought to be a newfound friend. The man who had worked so diligently as a volunteer!

"It's him, Daddy!" Bethany, her face

contorted with fear, pointed a shaky finger at Jim. "He's the one who took me away!"

Mindy raced toward her daughter, scooping her up in her arms and holding her close to her breast, barely noticing when Bethany winced in pain. "Oh, Bethany, my Bethany. My poor, poor baby!"

"He told me you'd sent him to pick me up at school that night because you'd had a car wreck. I believed him! He tied my hands together and took me to that awful place!"

"You did that to my daughter?" It was all Chuck could do to keep from wrapping his fingers around the man's neck and choking the life out of him.

"He — he told me that if anyone found me before he came back for me and I told them he was the one who had taken me —" Gasping for breath, Bethany stopped and stared at Jim. "He said he would kill both of you! That's why I didn't want to answer that man last night."

"You lowlife! You don't deserve to live!" Chuck pulled back his arm and took a swing at the man, but one of the orderlies restrained him.

Within minutes he and the two orderlies had Jim's hands and feet secured with medical tape, immobilizing him.

A nurse hurried into the room. "We found

the guard in a storage room down the hall. He's unconscious."

Chuck shook his head with disgust, then bent over Jim and spit on him. "Someone call 911 and ask for Captain Wyatt. Tell him we've got our man."

"Well, you're certainly looking better," Dr. Born told Bethany as he came into her room the next morning, chart in hand. "Nice to see you're eating, but take it easy. Your tummy has been without food for a few days."

"How long before we can take her home?" Mindy asked.

"Probably tomorrow. She's much better today than when she was brought in last night. Her rib is going to give her fits for a while, and it will take a couple of weeks for her head to heal, but her bruises will soon fade, and she'll be fine." He gestured toward the door. "Why don't you two go have some breakfast while I check her over?"

Smiling, Bethany shooed them toward the door. "Yeah, Mama, you and Daddy go eat. I'll be okay. I'm not afraid anymore."

"What'd Jim have to say when they questioned him?" Mindy asked as she and Chuck moved into the hall outside Bethany's room. "You haven't had a chance to tell me since you got back from the police station."

Chuck rolled his eyes. "I'm glad you weren't there to hear it. When confronted with the evidence, the guy actually spilled his guts, almost as if he was proud of what he'd done. Captain Wyatt said it was because he was hoping to plea bargain by giving the FBI the names of the people who mail him child porn."

"I can't believe he got Bethany to go with him."

"Agent Rogers said these guys spend days planning something like this. It seems one time when Bethany had stopped by the Porters' house to play with their dog, she told them how she and her friends talked to one another on that instant-message thing. She even told them the code name she used. Jim got on his computer and began talking to her as —"

"Trustworthy!" Mindy shook her head in disbelief.

"Yep, Trustworthy. He even admitted he was the one who left that bracelet in our flowerbed. Remember how in her diary she mentioned she'd told Trustworthy she wouldn't be able to talk to him that evening because she'd be at that play rehearsal? He knew exactly what time it would be over, and he was sitting in his car waiting when she came out of the school, hoping he could get to her and convince her to get in his car before you got there."

"But how could he be in two places at once? Everyone we knew, including the Porters, were questioned as to their whereabouts that evening. Janine swore he was at home with her all evening, watching a football game."

"That's the sad part. Janine had no idea her husband was involved in anything like this. He had fixed her a cup of hot cocoa laced with three high-powered sleeping pills. Then, once she dozed off, he slipped out and went to the school. She actually woke up just as he was coming in the front door after he'd taken Bethany to Bristol, but he said he'd been able to convince her he'd just stepped out onto the porch because he'd heard a noise out front and had gone to investigate."

Mindy closed her eyes, gulping hard. "Why — why did he want to take Bethany since he didn't — didn't — ?" She couldn't say the word.

"He planned to, but he knew he had to get back before his wife woke up. So he took her out to that old shed, meaning to come back the next day and do it. He'd even called a friend on his cell phone while he was driving, pretending to be at home watching the game, so he'd have that as a second alibi, in case he needed it later. But you know what? I think Bethany's prayers were what kept him from coming back. God was protecting her from further harm. I should have been suspicious when the guy spent so many hours passing out those flyers and putting up posters and the way he was constantly at my side, asking questions about the investigation. Especially when he made up that grid and didn't assign any of the volunteers to search the area where Bethany was found!"

"That's hindsight, Chuck. There's no way you could have known. Don't blame yourself. He had us all fooled."

He let out a heavy sigh. "That's what Captain Wyatt said."

It took Mindy a few minutes to absorb it all. "While you were gone, Bethany told me he had tried to pull her shirt off, but she hit at him and kicked him real hard — right where they told her to in the self-defense classes she took at school. It made him so angry he kicked her back several times with the toe of his boot, then grabbed up a piece of an old barrel stave and hit her with it — once across her ribs and the last time over her head, knocking her to the ground. She said she thought if she just lay there, he'd think she was dead. When she finally opened her eyes, he was gone, and the door was padlocked."

"Yeah, he told them he'd hit her and how she'd fallen to the floor with blood gushing from her wound and running down her face. He did think maybe he'd killed her, but he decided to leave her there and come back later. He never expected her to fight the way she did. I guess that kick of hers really hurt the guy — in the right place."

"I feel sorry for Janine. She told me she'd only known Jim for about two weeks before they got married."

"Yeah, I guess she was the one who messed up his plans to go back. She was so scared, with a crazed kidnapper on the loose, that she stuck to him like glue, and he couldn't shake her off long enough to drive back down to Bristol without raising suspicion. Agent Rogers said he asked Jim if he'd kidnapped any other girls. He laughed and said that was for them to find out. But when they confronted him with a number of pictures of young girls they'd found in his house, he actually bragged about the number he'd molested, most of them too embarrassed to let their parents or the authorities know. The FBI is hoping, armed with the pictures found in Jim's house and the information he has given them, that some of the other missing children's cases may be solved. Jim had met most of the girls on the Internet. Our precious, innocent, naive little girl has been at the mercy of this cunning, lecherous pervert for weeks, and we didn't even know it."

Mindy reached out and touched her husband's arm, then bowed her head. "Thank You, God, for keeping our baby safe while she was in the hands of that madman."

"Amen." Chuck pulled her hand to his lips and kissed it tenderly, gazing at her with eyes full of love. "Isn't it amazing the way God not only brought our Bethany back to us, but cleared my name as well, and I ended up with a big promotion?"

Mindy released a slight giggle. "I tried to help clear your name, Chuck. I did a bit of sleuthing on my own, but I wasn't very good at it."

Chuck tilted her face upward. "You? Sleuthing? How? What did you do?"

Mindy could not contain a full-fledged chuckle as she remembered what she had done and how foolish it seemed looking back on it. "I paid a visit to Clarisse and got her to pull up Michelle's file on her computer screen."

He reared back, his jaw dropping. "Clarisse gave you information on Michelle? That kind of stuff is confidential! I can't believe she gave it to you!"

"She didn't exactly give it to me. She left the room for a few minutes, and I copied it down myself."

"So? Did you find anything?"

"Not really. Nothing of any use."

"What exactly do you mean — nothing of any use?"

A smile curled at Mindy's lips. "I went Dumpster-diving in her trash."

Chuck's jaw dropped as he threw his arms into the air. "You what?"

"I pulled a big plastic bag out of her trash and took it home with me. It was a dumb thing to do. I actually sifted through Michelle's garbage. It was disgusting!"

Laughing, Chuck grabbed her up in his arms. "My prissy little Mindy — Dumpster-diving? Now that is a picture!"

"I guess I naively hoped I'd find a note or a scratch pad where she'd written some heinous plan to discredit your name. I wanted to prove your innocence. I may not have acted like it, but I loved you!"

Chuck let out a belly laugh as he lifted her and whirled her around the hospital corridor. "Dumpster-diving. I never would have believed it!"

"Michelle's gone, and I'm the new sales manager, Mindy! Can you believe it?"

Mindy leaned into Chuck's embrace. She had her family back, and it felt so good. "Yes, dearest, I can believe it. This week has been filled with miracles." She let her expression go somber. "But I think we should keep this to ourselves. There's no reason for Bethany to know about your suspension. She has enough to deal with."

The feeling of Chuck's lips on hers was delicious as he bent and kissed her. "I love you, Mindy O'Connor."

"I love you, too."

CHAPTER TWELVE

"Is my hair okay? Do I have on enough lipstick?" Mindy asked as she and Chuck sat on their sofa, staring into the lens of the portable TV video camera.

"You look beautiful, sweetheart."

"Heads up. We're ready." The WKRI-TV videographer behind the camera began his countdown, "Five, four, three, two, one," then pointed a finger at them.

"Hello, I'm Chuck O'Connor, and this is my wife, Mindy. Our daughter, Bethany, was kidnapped this past week and held captive for several days. But thanks to God, she has been found and is now home with us."

A bundle of nerves, Mindy cleared her throat and took a deep breath. "We want to thank all of you for your assistance in finding our daughter. Some by praying, some by actually helping in the search. We're fortunate. Our child has been returned to us. Many families are still waiting for news of their child." Mindy stared directly into the camera lens, speaking from her heart. "Cherish each minute you have with your children. Tell them how much you love them as often as you can. None of us knows what a day may bring."

Chuck gave her hand a squeeze as he took over. "If you have any information about a missing child, please call the Missing Children's hotline at 1-800-THE-LOST. Your information could be the lead that brings a child home to their anxious, waiting family. Thank you."

"Cut!"

Captain Wyatt gave them a smile. "You both did great. From what I've been told, your public service announcement will run not only in Rhode Island, but also in a number of the surrounding states. It may be the means of bringing other missing children home to their parents."

Chuck slipped an arm around Mindy. "We're both praying it will be."

Two days later Chuck stood in the middle of their family room, rubbing his chin and looking thoughtful. "I still don't understand one thing. How did that rag with Bethany's blood on it get into the trash barrel in our garage?"

"You mean that piece of your old shirt?" Bethany asked from her place on the sofa, looking surprised. "I put it there."

Mindy frowned. "When? You never bother the things on Daddy's workbench!"

"Tracie and I were skateboarding, and one of those boltie things in the bottom of my board was loose. I went to Daddy's workbench and got one of those wrenchie-type things and tried to tighten it; but my hand slipped, and I cut myself. I wiped the blood on Daddy's old shirt and put it in the trash. I didn't think I'd get in trouble for it. I didn't mess up Daddy's toolbox, and I put the wrench back where it was supposed to be."

Chuck raced to his daughter. "You're not in trouble, Princess. In fact, if it wasn't for your broken rib, I'd give you a big bear hug!"

"Your dad and I have an idea. We want your opinion. What would you think about us renewing our vows?"

The girl screwed up her face. "What does that mean?"

"Getting married again. We eloped the first time, and neither Grandma Carson or Grandma O'Connor got to attend our wedding," Chuck explained. "It wasn't much of a wedding. No one was there except the man who married us and his wife and some woman who played the organ."

"I didn't even have real flowers," Mindy confessed with a laugh. "I had a silk bouquet. I still have it, though it's probably a bit dusty. It's been up in the attic all these years."

"Wow! Some of my friends got to go to their mother's or father's wedding 'cause they got divorced and married someone else. But they've never been to their own parents' wedding. I think that'd be cool!"

"We've already talked to Pastor Park about it. He's going to perform the ceremony in three weeks," Mindy said with a loving glance toward her husband. "I want you to be my bridesmaid."

Bethany's eyes sparkled. "Really? A bridesmaid? Wow!"

"We'll have to buy you a new dress for it, but I'm going to try to get into the champagne-colored lace dress I wore at our first wedding. That dress cost me a whole two weeks' salary!"

Bethany clapped her hands together. "Wow! I can't wait to tell Tracie. Me — a bridesmaid!"

Mindy gazed at her daughter as she lay on the sofa covered up with the Jacob's Ladder quilt. "Are you sure you're up to this, sweetie? You've been through quite an ordeal. We don't want to push you. The wedding can be put off until —"

"No! I'm doing okay, honest. I want you and Daddy to get married!"

Mindy stroked her daughter's beautiful, silky hair. "Go call Tracie. Maybe she'd like to be a candlelighter."

"I will in a minute, but Daddy and I have a surprise for you." Bethany gave her father an exaggerated wink. "Could you get it for me, Daddy?"

With a mischievous smile exploding across his face, Chuck snapped his fingers, then hurried out of the room.

Mindy cocked her head to one side and frowned. "What was that all about?"

Bethany let out a giggle. "You'll see."

Chuck sauntered back into the family room and knelt in front of Mindy. "Bethany and I did a little shopping a couple of weeks ago, didn't we, Princess?"

A wide smile blanketed their child's sweet face.

"This is for you, with all our love." Chuck handed Mindy a small red-velvet jewelry box. "Sorry, we didn't wrap it."

She glanced from one smiling face to the other.

Bethany's eyes sparkled. "It's for Mother's

Day! I'm sorry we couldn't give it to you then."

With trembling fingers and a heart over-flowing with love, Mindy lifted the lid. "Oh! A gold locket! It's beautiful!"

"Daddy and I picked it out," Bethany said with pride, her face beaming. "You can wear it to your wedding! Look inside."

Carefully using the tip of her fingernail, Mindy popped it open. "Oh, pictures of the two people I love the most in all the world. You and your daddy." A tear clouded her vision.

"Do you like it, Mama?"

Mindy smiled at her daughter. "No, baby, I love it!"

Bethany cradled herself up next to Mindy. "I love you, Mama. Happy Mother's Day."

The next three weeks flew by as Mindy and Bethany shopped for Bethany's dress, arranged for flowers, called the caterer, and performed an array of other tasks necessary to plan a wedding.

While on a business trip to Providence, Chuck ran into an old friend, Keene Moray, an opera singer who had quit the opera to sing full-time for the Lord, and asked him to sing at their wedding. Knowing Keene's busy schedule, he'd expected him to say he wouldn't be able make it; but to his amazement the man agreed and even said he'd be bringing his wife, Jane.

Mindy shrieked when he told her Keene had accepted his invitation. "Keene Moray! The famous Keene Moray is going to sing at our wedding?" She threw her arms around Chuck's neck and, giggling like a schoolgirl, planted dozens of kisses all over his face.

"Wow! I'd have asked him long ago if I'd known I was going to get this kind of treatment!"

Finally, the day arrived. "I'm going to throw my bouquet to you, Treva. You need the love of a good man," Mindy told her friend as they stood before the mirror in the bride's room of the church.

Treva laughed out loud, then handed Mindy the bouquet of yellowed silk flowers from Chuck and Mindy's first wedding. "You think catching a bouquet of flowers will snag me a man?"

Mindy cocked her head coyly. "Well, you do have to do your part. You can't just sit and wait for him to come knocking on your door. You have to get out there and circulate."

"Circulate, huh? I'll give that piece of

advice some serious thought." She lifted the bouquet and touched one of its blossoms. "Hey, these silk flowers don't look too bad, considering they're fourteen years old. But I know they're precious to you, so if I catch them, I promise to give them back to you so you can save them for Bethany."

To Mindy's surprise, every seat in the church sanctuary was filled, as friends, church members, Bethany's teachers and classmates, both Chuck and Mindy's business associates, and countless volunteers who had helped find Bethany crowded into the pews.

Mindy's joy was uncontainable as she stood between her handsome husband and her beautiful daughter, listening to the rich baritone voice of Keene Moray as he sang the words of "I Love You Truly," which had been sung at their first wedding.

God had blessed her more abundantly than she could ever ask or imagine He would. *How quickly life can change. In the twinkling of an eye,* Mindy thought as she held tightly to her husband's arm, *the things I've taken for granted — the most precious things in my life — were nearly taken from me. I came so close to losing both my husband and my daughter. But thanks to God's goodness and His everlasting love, I didn't, and my little family has been reunited.*

She wiped away a tear of joy with her gloved hand and listened carefully as Pastor Park challenged the two of them to live for God and for each other, and in her heart of hearts she knew she'd found her calling.

With a warm smile Pastor Park took Mindy's hand and placed it in Chuck's. "By the power vested in me by the state of Rhode Island, I now pronounce you husband and wife. You may kiss your bride."

A tingle ran through Mindy as Chuck slowly lifted her veil; then, gazing into her face with eyes filled with love, he kissed her. This time, though, it was different from when he'd kissed her in the little wedding chapel in Las Vegas. Now they were experienced adults who had faced tremendous challenges in their lives, not silly twenty-year-olds with pie-in-the-sky ideas. And they knew, without a shadow of a doubt, their love was real and would last a lifetime.

"I love you, my darling," Chuck whispered against her lips. "I'll love you forever, and I promise always to be there for you."

"I love you, too, sweetheart. With God as my witness, I'll strive to be the best wife I can be. The wife you deserve."

As Mindy felt a small hand slip into hers, she pulled away from Chuck's embrace.

Bending, she kissed Bethany's shining face. "And I love you, too, baby. Thanks for praying for us. Your faith is what brought us here."

As the organ began to play, Chuck grabbed Mindy's hand, then reached out his free hand toward Bethany. "Come on, Princess. We want you with us."

Mr. and Mrs. Chuck O'Connor and their daughter, Bethany, together again, walked down the aisle to begin life anew — this time with God as the head of their family.

Dear Reader,

I love Rhode Island! It is always a joy when I get a chance to visit there. It's a beautiful state filled with some of the nicest people you'll ever meet. If you haven't been there, I hope these three stories will whet your appetite and make you want to go. On our first trip to Rhode island, we toured four of Newport's famous mansions. I remember walking and gawking through those lovely homes with my mouth gaping open. What luxury! What opulence! Yet when you hear the stories of those who lived in some of those museum-like houses, their beauty fades. So much misery, strife, deceit, and family bickering took place, it makes you wonder if some of those people ever truly had a happy day. I'd much prefer to live in the mansion our heavenly Father is preparing for us. How about you!

How I wish you and I could sit down

together, sip glasses of iced tea, and just visit. I would love to know all about you — your joys, your sorrows, your ups and downs, what inspires you, and how God is working in your life. I remember how my grandmother and grandfather used to spend every evening sitting on their front porch visiting with neighbors, waving at the pass-ersby, and enjoying their time with one another. No pressures, no TV to distract them, no cell phone. Sounds good, doesn't it? It seems we're so busy these days, the average family has trouble just scheduling one night a week when they all can have dinner together. I'm so thankful for those wonderful unrushed family times Don and I had with our children when they were growing up. Nothing can replace the time we spend together. So many people don't find that out until it is too late.

As many who read my books know, my precious husband went home to be with the Lord several years ago. Don was (and is) my inspiration for the hero of every book I write. I dedicate this book to him, the love of my life.

Joyce Livingston

A NOTE FROM THE AUTHOR

I love to hear from my readers! You may correspond with me by writing:

**Joyce Livingston
Author Relations
PO Box 719
Uhrichsville, OH 44683**

ABOUT THE AUTHOR

Joyce Livingston has done many things in her life (in addition to being a wife, mother of six, and grandmother to oodles of grandkids, all of whom she loves dearly), from being a television broadcaster for eighteen years, to lecturing and teaching on quilting and sewing, to writing magazine articles on a variety of subjects. She's danced with Lawrence Welk, ice-skated with a chimpanzee, had bottles broken over her head by stuntmen, interviewed hundreds of celebrities and controversial figures, and done many other interesting and unusual things. But now, when she isn't off traveling to wonderful and exotic places as a part-time tour escort, her days are spent sitting in front of her computer, creating stories. She feels her writing is a ministry and a calling from God, and she hopes Heartsong readers will be touched and uplifted by what she writes. Joyce loves to hear from her readers and invites you to visit her on the Internet at www.joycelivingston.com.